I0525972

Song of the Arrow

Also in this series of new poetry and fiction from LinguaBooks

Tales from Happy Valley
A Parting Shot
Belongings
No Means No
The Legend of Sidora
The Taste of Rain

For more information, go to www.linguabooks.com

Song of the Arrow

An Otherworld Adventure

Michael Griffiths

LinguaBooks
www.linguabooks.com

All rights reserved. No part of this publication may be reproduced, stored in a retrieval system or transmitted, in any form or by any means, electronic, mechanical, photocopying, recording or otherwise, without the prior permission of the publishers.

Paperback edition: ISBN 978-1-916511-04-0
eBook edition: ISBN 978-1-916511-05-7

First edition

Editor: Ann Claypole

Copyright © 2025 LinguaBooks

A CIP catalogue record for this book is available from the British Library.

Michael Griffiths has asserted his right under the Copyright, Designs and Patents Act, 1988 to be identified as the author of this work.

This book is sold subject to the condition that it shall not, by way of trade or otherwise, be lent, resold, hired out or otherwise circulated without the publisher's prior consent in any form of binding or cover other than that in which it is published and without a similar condition including this condition being imposed on the subsequent purchaser.

This is a work of fiction. Any resemblance to actual persons, living or dead, or actual events is purely coincidental.

LinguaBooks
Elsie Whiteley Innovation Centre
Hopwood Lane
Halifax HX1 5ER
www.linguabooks.com

Life is infinitely stranger than anything which the mind of man could invent.

— Arthur Conan Doyle

To Alison

thank you

Preface

This is not a book. It's a song. An enchanted air from the Otherworld. It is the sound an arrow makes as it flies towards your heart.

Many of the events described took place some forty-seven years ago, but I remember them as vividly as if they had actually happened. Others are recent and hence more difficult to summon clearly.

I have recorded both here to the best of my recollection. All of which is in keeping with my core belief; life is a brief walk between baths.

Michael Griffiths, Hebden Bridge, March 2025

Part One

Wivenhoe Park, Colchester, 1980

I

Students were not allowed to swim in the lake. The signpost that told them this had been placed at one of the points which allowed the easiest access to disobedience. Now on this unseasonably hot day in early June, many would take full advantage of its cooling properties by stripping off, treading through the thick, cloying mud and slipping into its comforting softness.

I remembered the feel of the rough silt between my toes and could imagine the feeling of release as arms and then shoulders sank into its silky embrace. A dozen or more students had already surrendered themselves to such enticements. I wouldn't be joining them. I had a book to read, a book I should have read back in October, a book that explained where my studies in literature should have been leading throughout this, my second year at university. Even at the tail-end of the nineteen seventies most students my age had a better attitude to study. I had mastered the art of turning up to the weekly tutorials and speaking about various books which I hadn't read as though I'd actually attended the lectures. Miraculously, I'd managed to get all my work in by the absolute deadline, and now faced the end of year exams. It's not easy writing essays on things you haven't read, even when they're sat in front of you. In an exam setting it's really tricky.

So today I couldn't swim. I couldn't join the numberless groups of friends, drinking, smoking, having fun on this beautiful afternoon. It had only just passed noon, and some were eating what they'd been able to pool together as improvised picnics. I had no time for hunger. I had to read. Yet wherever I sat on the lawns around the lake I found that someone would come and join me; or else they'd lean over while walking past, inviting me to join their group instead of sitting on my own and frowning.

I would have gone back to my very small student room, but that was no guarantee of quiet or freedom from disturbance, and I needed both. Such a wonderful day. Such a waste. I needed to be alone with the book. Then I saw it, a tree. An oak, as I now know it to be. The lowest leaf-frilled branches stretched out from its trunk about three yards above the ground. I thought that if I could get up there, they would provide a perfect place of refuge. I could see some stubby, knobbly, knuckly bits of tree that I felt would allow me to climb easily to this point.

I was wrong. I didn't discover how far apart some of the foot or handholds were until I'd already thrown my bag up into the cradle of the branches. I'd been carrying my pillow under my arm, and this too had been successfully lobbed into my intended hiding place. I'd quite wisely judged that it would be impossible for me to climb the trunk while holding onto these. After three attempts, all of which ended with me crashing to the ground, I considered the situation. I would need the pillow that night if I was to get any sleep before exam day. The blasted book was in the bag. So I kept trying, and after wiping dust and grass stains twice more from my hands, I finally managed it.

I sat in the branches, breathing heavily. I looked down upon the animated conversations going on nearby; from up here I heard nothing of the chatter. The tree was large, spreading a dappled arc across the grass, but this early in the summer no-one wanted to sit in its shade. Bringing my attention back to my immediate surroundings, I noticed a little arched hollow in the trunk, right next to where I sat. Peering inside, it seemed that the tree had grown a perfectly natural interior of benches, a table, and ever further receding doorway arches within. It made me smile to think of a squirrel enjoying such a seemingly human habitat.

Feeling I should acknowledge my trespass, I felt in my pocket and found what looked like a newly minted silver-coloured coin. I whimsically left it as payment to the squirrel, or magpie perhaps, and I read my book. I read it in a way I've never read anything before or since. It all made perfect sense. I understood, not just how this past year's study programme had been arranged, but how the entire history of literature was a quest for truth and beauty. I could see how every great storyteller on the course, Chaucer, Shakespeare, Dante, Milton, fitted into that tradition. It placed me firmly in the middle of a literary spiral reaching back beyond the written word, because its centre is everywhere.

When I next looked about me, the park was deserted. It had grown cold, and twilight was giving everything a magical shimmer. I again thanked the tree and its inhabitants and carefully allowed my bag and pillow to fall to the ground. Getting down was much quicker than the climb up, but I'm not sure it was easier. I hung by my fingers from the lowest branch and dropped the last yard or so, landing first on my feet, and then with a thump on my backside.

I heard laughter. I looked about but there was no-one there. I picked up my things and started back toward the accommodation block. Again I heard laughter. It was now getting properly dark, and the full moon had begun to gift me a shadow. I turned back to where the sound had come from and beneath the oak sat a large group of hippies. More laughter.

"He thinks we're students." The words weren't mine, but they were in my head.

"What are you then?" I asked myself.

"Faeries," was the answer. Never in a hundred lifetimes would I have thought that the tall, slim figures before me could be described in this way.

"You can't be Faeries," I thought. I heard laughter, mocking me. "OK. Faeries then. But you can't be real."

Again laughter, this time like they were really letting go. I looked around me, but apart from these revellers no-one was in sight.

"Could other people see you?" I asked aloud.

Still the answer was only in my head, and it took the form of a question: "Can you *see* other people?"

I wasn't really sure whether this required an answer, so I got clever: "How can you prove that you're real?"

This was greeted with the longest and loudest peal of laughter yet. I realised how truly ridiculous my question was. Then two of them that had been lying together flew effortlessly off into the air, still entwined in what looked like a lover's embrace. I was shocked.

"How did you do that?"

Another two, this time seated, also became airborne. Now I've always wanted to fly. I used to, in my dreams. I have aerial views of the Calder

Valley where I grew up etched in my memory. From up there the raked, stone houses look almost insignificant. The overwhelming impression is of a wilderness of trees, and even the roads seem as natural as the river Calder itself.

"Could I fly with you?" I pleaded.

Two cross-legged figures, both male, floated to my sides and gripped my elbows. For an instant I thought that I was about to join them in the sky. Then I realised it was just me trying to assist the process by standing on tiptoe. Laughing they flew away, legs uncrossing as one pretended to playfully escape, the other to catch his mate. More than a little crestfallen, I began to walk slowly around the tree. Then I saw her.

To say this was the most beautiful woman I had ever seen would be to exalt these words to a height never before achieved. Beauty, woman, sight; all were inadequate expressions with which to describe this experience. I didn't just see her, I felt every inch, every second, every tremor of life as if it were my own. I knew that my heart was lost. I had no choice but to do whatever she might ask of me. Then I saw, sitting in front of this tall and elegant sylph, another so far exceeding the first in beauty that it was painful. All I wanted was to declare my love, to offer to serve her all my days. I noticed that this second figure was brushing the flowing hair of a recumbent female in front of her. As the silver hairbrush was lowered, I saw that framed within those dark tresses was a paragon of loveliness. I could have died. I thought perhaps I had, for this was certainly a goddess. I fell to my knees and bowed my head.

"Come closer," like the whisper of a soft breeze. I looked up and she was staring straight at me. Her eyes, even in the dark, were brilliant, surely the moonlight actually came from them. They moved seas, progressed the seasons, imprisoned souls.

"Please," I begged, "what can I give you?" Without any command to do so, I took off my shoes and socks and walked hesitantly towards her. Every one of the Faeries had fallen silent, and all eyes were on her. There was a hush of expectation, and I knew, somehow, that she could crush me with a gesture. Her fingers quivered, gathering a handful of air, and the night was filled with the most extraordinary music. It was as if the earth, trees and lake had harmonised with the most joyous dawn chorus imaginable. All of those assembled began to line up in an avenue towards the three sisters, who remained motionless at the foot of the tree. The oak somehow seemed a greater distance away now, and as I walked towards it, the tree receded even further. Starting to run, I became aware that the ground was inclining downward. My last impression of this world was of tangled roots, like the arch of a gateway above my head. And I was in darkness.

II

"What's the matter, afraid of the dark?"

The thought could very easily have been my own, but it wasn't. It was more playful, less critical than mine would have been. I say "thought" but it's quite strange, and worth pointing out, that these thoughts had all the characteristics of speech. Amongst them differing voices could be discerned; and the rhythm, intonation and timbre was in every case unique. This voice I'd heard before.

"Do you have a name?" I asked.

"I have, but it's not one to be spoken aloud."

In my imagination I pictured a tree that grew stronger the more it endured. Like water, it did this by becoming not harder but more pliant. As it bent to the wind, I heard a murmur in the leaves. It seemed to whisper Alder. Alfric. Alethea. The voice claimed a host of such names. Many of these were ancient, arcane, or even completely unpronounceable.

"Just call me Al," it said.

I had fallen so easily into the habit of not speaking aloud the reverberating echo of my laughter proved quite unnerving.

"Careful," said Al silently. "You might give away our presence."

Perhaps that's why they communicate like this, I thought, so as to stay safe from humans.

"Not humans," was the reply and through the words I could taste a sickness and a fear. Of course, I'm not actually afraid of the dark. Sometimes I've walked through woodland in pitch darkness. Once, after reading Carlos Castaneda, I'd even followed his advice to run with nothing to guide me, in a state of complete blind faith.

"That sounds fun." Al's thought had interrupted my own. I realised nothing in his company could truly be considered private. The path was sloping downwards and that had been the reason for my stopping. Gravity, unlike darkness, is a real force which can cause serious injury.

"Believe me," said Al, "darkness is a real force too." Something in his words awoke a terror in me that made it impossible to continue.

"Don't worry," said the voice in my head, but my body wasn't listening.

"Listen," said Al, "I'm with you, I won't leave you, I won't let you go."

"But I have to go back. There's an exam tomorrow."

Al knew this wasn't the real reason. His thoughts came to me slowly and with deliberation. "Not many people are given this chance to move between the worlds. If your choice is to go back, I'll take you. We're half way there. It's up to you." Part of me wanted to continue into the darkness, to discover what was on the other side of it. But my greatest anxieties were weighing on me.

"Change, uncertainty, and failure," thought Al, and there was something about the way he flicked the words into my head that made them lighter, almost laughable.

"How do you know that?" I asked silently.

Al continued with his encouragement. "The only person you need to worry about failing is yourself."

I realised then why the exam had seemed important to me. Mum, Dad, my old teachers at school, all had expectations. But it wasn't them I needed to please. For the first time in my life, I felt I could please myself. A great weight seemed to have left me.

"Thank you," I thought. For some reason a word I'd never really understood popped into my head. Friendship.

Soon the corridor began to lead upwards, and we quickened our pace. By the time we reached the top, we were almost jogging. Enough light came past the edges of an obstruction for me to see its arched shape, also something of its construction, which was in the nature of cleverly woven sticks or reeds. I could make out some leathery hinges, tied between the frame and the door itself. All of the smells around me, heightened by the absence of light and sound, had been earthy, subterranean, warm and dank. Now, though, I caught the scent of something altogether more inviting. Food.

When Al opened the entrance, I was completely unprepared for the sight and sound before me. The door didn't seem solid enough to have afforded any soundproofing, but no sooner was it ajar than I heard singing, laughing, the clattering of crockery and glassware, numerous white-noised conversations and everywhere happiness. No, not happiness, joy. I could see dozens of small groups in what could only be described as a Great Hall. Pillars of growing wood stretched up to the dark recesses of, I guess, a ceiling. Invisible not only because it was so high, but because the entire hall was lit by what at first I took to be a thousand tiny candles. Then I saw that the closest of these lights was simply floating in the air with no candle or other energy source to be seen.

"You must have heard of Faerie Lights," laughed Al.

But these, while resembling Christmas-tree lights in the way they twinkled and sparkled, and also in their myriad colours, were altogether more magical. I remembered hearing carols sung by children at Christingle services back in Calderdale. I wiped away the tears.

So far Al had been only a voice in my head, an inclination, a feeling. Looking at him for the first time should have given me my first impression. The fact it didn't was probably a good thing. He was taller than me, better looking, and had a natural grace and confidence. I would probably have taken an instant dislike to him. The darkness had allowed me to see Al more clearly and also perhaps to be a truer version of myself.

"You still miss her then?" Al had seen right to the source of my emotion in a way that I have struggled to admit. I was embarrassed to be so unshielded from another.

"Help yourself to food," he said, "it *will* help."

Heartsease. I heard the word in my head. I had no idea that the tiny blooms in front of me went by that name. But I took Al's word for it. Along the table between all the enchanting dishes of food were the most delicate, fluted glasses. They were miniscule, yet only half filled with a liquid that glimmered in the flickering rhythm of the magical lighting. Inside each glass, an elegant display of wildflowers had been arranged. Violet, speedwell, forget-me-not, tansy, corn flowers, poppy, viola, pansy, daffodil, daisy, orchid, iris, buttercup, columbine, bellflower, lilacs. And the food! I had never seen dishes of such intricate variety. There were breads, cakes, biscuits and pies of every imaginable shape and size. Tarts, sweet or savoury, displayed fruits and vegetables of rich colour and texture. Cheeses teased my sense of smell so that it was all that I could do not to reach for them. But no, I would be a well-mannered guest and let Al serve himself first.

"I've eaten already. Just help yourself," so saying, he walked off to a group that was patently delighted to see him.

I picked up a plain white plate and set about decorating it with enthusiasm, for I was suddenly ravenously hungry. Sniffing the intoxicating aroma of some latticed strips of still-warm pastry, adorned with beetroot puree and fragrant blue cheese, it was all I could do to continue without sampling them immediately. I placed two onto my plate and then wished I hadn't, for now I would have less room for the freshest green salad I had ever seen. Moist pea shoots, romaine lettuce, parsley, dill, sage, chives, mint and rosemary all assailed my senses. The plate was soon brimming over with nuts, fruits, pastries and salads. I looked about me for somewhere to sit and enjoy the feast.

"Don't eat the food," I heard someone whisper. I mean I really heard it, not in my head but aloud. I turned and saw a middle-aged man, slightly balding. He looked out of place in this company of long-haired, youthful merrymakers.

"Don't drink anything either," again, a whisper. I saw that he was deliberately not looking at me and was trying to say this with as little movement of the lips as possible. His sharp eyes darted at me for a second and I saw a kindness and concern which made me trust him despite his long sideburns and slightly hawkish eyes. I noticed he had food.

"It's too late for me, I'm already under the enchantment." I was more than a little frightened as I realised that he must have heard my thoughts. Confused too; could he really be human?

"Aye lad, that I am but I've been here a long time." There was a sadness in his voice. "I can hear your thoughts clear enough, but I can't think in a way that would allow you to hear mine. However, all that might change if you eat or drink anything." I started to put my plate down on the table, intending to push it away from me. "No," he urged, "they'll notice, just mingle."

Anyone who's been given food at a children's party or a lugubrious buffet has learnt the art of mingling without grazing. You pick something up from your plate, talk a while with someone, all the time pretending to be too polite to speak and eat at the same time, then move on. In between people, or groups of people, food can be returned to the table and another item selected. But this wasn't some sad-looking display; this was the most enticing collection of dainties I had ever beheld. Resisting was tough, but that, I thought, is precisely the point. The food is meant to look and smell like your heart's desire. I knew that if I tasted even a drop or a crumb, I would not be able to stop myself from stuffing my face.

"She will see you now." In Al's voice I heard something more than fear or respect. It was a tone of awe. I knew that whoever she was, there was no refusing her. I became suddenly very anxious; hot and cold at the same time, breathless and unfocused.

"Don't worry," said Al. "You've met the Queen already and she quite likes you."

III

I followed Al to a set of double doors at the far end of the Great Hall. On either side stood a Faerie larger than any I had yet seen, each armed with a six-foot long, silver-tipped spear. As we approached, they each took hold of something in the detail of the beautifully carved hardwood doors. Soundlessly these swung open to reveal a cloud of glittering dust. The motes of dust didn't so much catch the light, as set it free. Sunlight swirled and danced in a million intricate patterns, in colours that I am sure are beyond any rainbow. It was the most magical thing I had so far seen.

"So this is fairy dust," I thought. The laugh that I heard was like that of a mother watching a baby at play. Then an indulgent reprimand.

"There's no such thing silly, it's just dust." Again laughter. I turned in time to see an encouraging look from Al before the guards closed the door between us. The sound of the only exit being secured was a little too solid and final for my liking.

"Don't look so nervous," said a voice, "I won't bite." This thought was accompanied by a picture in my mind's eye of needle sharp and all too numerous teeth. Otherwise it might have been reassuring. Then the dust settled enough for me to behold a vision of loveliness. The Queen was the third of the women I had seen sitting under the tree. The one whose fearsome beauty led me to take off my socks and shoes. I looked down and felt embarrassed that I hadn't even remembered to pick them up.

"Just as well. You'd never have been allowed in to see me while wearing them."

"It's a great honour," I said.

"So it is. One you would have not been afforded but for your tribute." She gestured with her hand, the way she had earlier when summoning music, and my eyes had no choice but to follow her direction. This took my attention to the window through which the sunlight was streaming. How long have I been here? I wondered. It was only just dark when I entered but this much heat and light told me that now it must be at least midday.

"Time is different here," she explained. "More manageable." I thought she'd drawn my gaze to a large expanse of glittering silver just beyond the arched window. Then I realised what it was that I was admiring: the coin I had left in the branches of the tree. But now the tiny coin was about twelve or fifteen feet in diameter. "It takes a bit of getting used to," she said, sensing my discomfort. "Better not to think that you're really small, rather that there are two worlds each built to a different scale."

"But the dust, is it really just ordinary dust?"

"Oh yes, it's been around all of your life and it's not the first time it's moved like that in the sunlight. Only once before have you ever really seen it."

I remembered then being about four years old, maybe younger. My mother had put me in an armchair, imprisoned by cushions, while she spring-cleaned. It was a sunny day and as she flicked the duster here and there the air was painted with the most brilliant and enchanting particles of house-hold dust. I'd wanted to get out and play or dance amongst them but hadn't dared disobey my mother's instruction to stay put.

"You can dance now if you want to."

I smiled at the Queen's understanding.

Then she danced. She was the sea playing with the shore, the moon circling the night sky, a field of sunflowers turning towards the light and more, so much more. She was joy, sadness, mystery and magic. She was dance. Tears fell from my cheeks onto the dry oak floor.

"Another gift," she laughed, "how wonderful."

Now I too was caught up in her movement, swirling without effort or will, or self-consciousness in a way that I couldn't ever have dreamt of.

"This is reality - you're just not used to it."

I could have stayed there forever, might be there still, if the double doors hadn't suddenly swung open to reveal a violent chaos beyond. At once from a hundred different minds a word of horror, distress, revulsion came into my head: "goblins."

Sheer panic took hold of me. To protect the Queen was my first thought but she was already being spirited away through a hitherto unseen doorway into some deeper recess of the tree. As this secret door disappeared behind her, there came a new thought: survival. I wanted to hide, to run, to fight, and all of them at once.

"Fight," came the thought, but I cannot say for certain it was mine. A common bravery seemed to be sweeping through the Great Hall. Everyone, everywhere, was taking up a spear, a sword, a wooden club or a shield. They were moving to-wards the tunnel through which I had first entered the tree. Then, as if swept up by a ferocious tidal wave, they were all borne back toward me.

"Don't let them through," I heard myself shout. "Protect the Queen."

"Hummannss."

I felt a cold hiss enter my body through my ears which chilled me to the bone. For a moment I thought to hide or run away.

"Resist," Al was rallying the multitude. "Protect our home."

It was working. People, for now locked in combat they really did resemble humanity, were pushing, clubbing, slashing and defending. And doing so with a determination and ferocity that moments before I would have thought them incapable of descending into. And then it was over. There was no blood, no bodies, but lots of damage. Tables, chairs, food and flowers were strewn everywhere. A few of the Faerie folk seemed to have minor injuries and they were being held, rocked or nursed by friends or family.

Then a terrible thought was felt by all.

"Al," came the cry. "They've taken Al."

Part Two

The Shield and Mirror

IV

"We must mount a rescue mission," I pleaded for the umpteenth time.

The Queen sat, impassive, on a simple wooden throne which seemed to be a very part of the tree upon which it stood. I realised it was one of the little wooden chairs I'd seen through the arched hole all those hours before. The importance I'd attached to finding a place of peace to study the textbook now seemed so insignificant.

"We must rescue Al," I persisted.

"He is lost." It was a song of lament, of limitless loss and sadness.

"No!" I shouted silencing them. "He is my friend and I will bring him back." There was no laughter, but I could feel complete disbelief. I understood in that instant that none of them could accompany me, for they knew what the goblins would be doing to Al. They closed their thoughts off, eager that I should catch no glimpse of such cruelty. I should learn to close up like that, I thought. And they laughed at this, but not unkindly.

"I'd like to go too," said the balding man who had earlier warned me not to eat.

"You cannot leave this place." This came as a statement of fact from the Queen, not a command.

"Not even with Your Majesty's permission?" It was framed as a question, but I sensed that the real question was whether such permission would be granted. The Queen raised only an eyebrow, her head tilted to one side.

"Very well, Man-Ro. You may leave." Each word of this proclamation was equally stressed, and with every syllable it was as if the room got lighter and a little less real. "But be quick before I change my mind."

"Come on," he said, tugging my arm. "We'll need weapons."

When I had first entered the Great Hall with Al (how it pained me to think of him captured) I hadn't noticed the weapons. This is hardly surprising. Most Faerie implements are made of wood and blend in perfectly with the Great Trees in which they spend the hours of daylight. Now I could see that there were dozens of staffs, sticks, bows and spears, but that here and there stood out a glint of metal.

"Silver," said Manro, "they can't abide iron." I thought back to the leather hinges, the lack of cutlery, the absence of locks or key holes.

"Yes," he continued, "iron locks would come in handy against goblins, humans too perhaps, but it hurts them to be near such metals. I've heard tell of how an iron nail was once driven into the trunk of the tree, no doubt for some human to hang a sign. It caused such anguish to the whole kingdom. Then after several days it simply rusted and fell out, and once again they could sleep away the daylight hours."

"So are they nocturnal?" I asked aloud.

"Apparently they didn't used to be, but now there is little in the world above to please them except at night when most humans are asleep."

"Can we just take whatever weapons we want?" I was keen to return to the task in hand.

"What are you attracted to?" he asked. "What catches your eye?" My gaze had in fact been drawn to a mirror hung on a distant wall. Time and again it had caught my attention. I wondered why Faeries should think they would need such a thing. "Ah," said my companion. "The shield of reflection."

As we walked towards it, I could see that it wasn't a true mirror. At first it looked to be reflecting the room and indeed our approaching selves. Then as I got closer, I saw instead a great hairy brute framed within the shield, with hanging arms and greedy eyes. I glanced behind me, then back, and caught a glimpse of the brute's head doing likewise. His look, or rather my look of astonishment, made Manro laugh.

"It shows you as you really are," he said.

I tried to look away, but it was compelling. Eventually, I turned my back on it. Behind me I felt Manro approach and put into my left hand a leather covered handle. Looking down I could see that the back of the shield was made of simple wood.

"No," he said, "wood from the Tree. And silver poured by the ancients when the moon was still young."

"It can't be that old."

"It's how we describe each newborn moon here, but the silver's still pretty old. As is this." With those words he pulled down a very battered look-ing quarterstaff from where it had hung above the shield. Until now his movements had been slow, almost ponderous, which made me think him quite advanced in years. As soon as the staff was in his hands, he stepped lightly and very quickly from one foot to the other, twirled his stick nimbly about his back, over his head, and if I hadn't jumped he would surely have swept my legs from under me. The whole intricate manoeuvre had taken barely a second. Now his position looked as if he was lean-ing on it for support, but the glint in his eye said otherwise.

"Aaron's cudgel," he said, "older than the shield, this tree, or anything in the world above. It's good to feel its sap again."

I had been more than happy with my magical shield. It had felt deliciously powerful in my hand

and so much lighter than I would have imagined. But now I looked about me for something more and caught sight of what I thought was a casting of a silver fish. It stood atop a hazel wand about three foot in length.

"The Arrow of Truth," said Manro. "I don't think you'd like that one bit."

"I could have sworn its eye moved to look at me."

"Sounds as if it likes you. Mmmm." His brow was creased in thought. "Well, why not then? Let's see what you're made of."

"So where's the bow?" I asked.

He laughed. "It's a throwing arrow. And don't worry there's no need to practise, it always hits its target. That's the problem." It didn't sound like much of a problem to me. So without further preparation, we said goodbye to those wishing us success and set off to descend to the real world, weapons at the ready.

V

Upon stepping into the moonlight, I was surprised to find how much reflected light my shield was providing. As I turned back to the tree it made the shadow branches on the ground stretch out menacingly. It was as bright as a car headlamp.

"A what?" said Manro and for an instant into my mind was conjured an image of a coal miner with a candle fastened to his helmet. Then that of a vintage car's light box.

"Ah, one of those," said Manro.

Confused, I shook my head and carried on walking. Before long we were trying to prise our way through tousled undergrowth. At the far end of the university lake is a runnel which carries excess water to a nearby brook. Approaching this purposefully, Manro crossed it and headed for a particularly thick patch of brambles. He spun his stick and the thorn bush parted enough to reveal a wet and uninviting hole set in the rocks that form the boundary of the lake.

"Wait for me!" I shouted, but Manro had already disappeared into the dark recess. I had to get on my hands and knees to squeeze myself into the opening. Manro was striding ahead. "Come on," he whispered urgently.

His staff, although almost a head and shoulders above my own height, wasn't even scraping the ceiling. Ignoring my fear, I jumped to my feet and ran after him. The entrance behind me was the last thing I saw before turning a bend. I noticed that it was the same diameter as the rest of the tunnel. "We've shrunk again!" I thought, but I hadn't felt a thing.

Some sort of illumination would have been reassuring. Unlike the tunnel to the Great Hall, this one just kept going down. It became ever darker, warmer and smelt, very strongly, of something unfamiliar. I began to hear guttural voices and caught some kind of smoke in the air which hurt the back of my throat. We were about to turn a second corner made visible by a flickering red light when a couple of startled eyes, large and round, appeared in front of us. In the dark I could see nothing else until two rows of sharp, fish-like teeth appeared. I felt a whoosh of air as Manro moved swiftly and I heard a "thunk" as eyes, teeth and presumably the rest of the goblin hit the ground.

"Careful now," said Manro quietly. "Don't raise the alarm when you step over him."

If I'd been able to think back at him, I would have pointed out that my alarm was already raised to a pretty deafening level. I knew something was preventing such communication down here, but my laboured breathing or perhaps even my heartbeat was enough to betray my state of fear.

"Calm yourself lad."

I did so and putting the image of those teeth behind me, walked briskly on. Manro came to a halt so abruptly that I nearly crashed into him. In front of us was a large cavern. Stalactites hung down in hideous fashion, like the giant fangs of a snake. There were half a dozen large smoking torches set in the middle of the chamber around a ghost-like seated figure. The hair hung lank and sweaty, the skin was almost translucent and the expression on this apparition was one of limitless dismay. Then I noticed that the figure was bound, wrist and ankle, by manacles chained to the heavy iron throne upon which they were sat. Studying their appearance more closely, I realised that this was Al. I let out a little cry.

"Hummannsss," echoed a deep voice.

From the shadows there emerged dozens of hunched figures, all scurrying towards us. Manro sprang into action and several toppled, holding bruised arms, or shins, or battered heads. Some who fell didn't move at all afterwards, but I think they were only knocked out. One ran straight at me and got so close I could smell his stinking breath. I feared for my life. Luckily some instinct took over and I swung the shield in front of me. He let out a piteous cry and fell to the floor sobbing. I turned the shield towards other fast-approaching goblins. It had a similar effect. Then I heard what the one on his knees in front of me was saying between sobs.

"Sooo sorry, been a bad gobbo, done a bad thing. Gobbo so bad. So ugly. Can't look. Forgive Gobbo." Tears fell onto the cavern floor as his chin juddered up and down. I felt sorry for him, until I remembered that the only thing causing him to feel like this was seeing the image of his own true form. With all the goblins now incapacitated or fleeing, Manro strode purposefully to the throne. He struck the chains repeatedly with his staff. This had no effect but to create sparks where the iron met the stone floor.

"Is there a key?" he asked, but Al was in such distress that the question didn't seem to register at all. I felt he wasn't even aware of us being there.

"Al," I tried. "It's me, Robyn," and maybe there was the faintest of glimmers in his wide, unfocused eyes.

"We need the keys," said Manro and he began looking about the cavern, but with no real sense of purpose or hope of success.

A huge dark shadow appeared on the wall in front of me. I turned towards the passage down which many of the horde had fled. There was a dreadful stench, as if of burnt wool or rotting meat: and the sound of very large feet slapping the cold stone, ever closer, in a slow deliberate step.

"The Goblin King," said Manro, "perhaps he'll have a key."

Imagine the most hideous, wart encrusted, bilious creature that you can. Think of it lumbering toward you, eight foot tall and almost as wide. The stench is unbearable, the fear primordial, as you see reptilian lids closing sideways over sulphur-yellow eyes. With a roar of hungry rage it springs, and you know that even if you could move, even if you could remember how to move, you would not be quick enough to escape its slathering jaws.

Suddenly Manro was there, in front of me, the cudgel held high. He brought the great staff crashing down squarely on my assailant's head. It blinked once and with a prehensile claw batted the man aside as if he were a ball of dry grass. Then slowly, deliberately, the monstrous form began to inch towards me. For a moment it looked apprehensive, and I remembered the Arrow of Truth. As I levelled it to my chin, the terrible creature shrank slightly away. Forgetting this dart always hits home, I took careful aim before releasing it into the screaming, juddering void. The Goblin King was gone. At first, I thought that the weapon would return to my hand, like a boomerang, but as it circled it seemed to pick up speed and was now heading straight at me. I felt it pierce my heart. I think I may have prayed. I certainly closed my eyes. That's instinct I guess, when you see something about to hit your chest. And it did, I felt it. I was aware of it passing right through me and in its passing, it left a feeling of enormous relief.

"You've hardly changed at all." I opened my eyes to see Manro's quizzical face, very close to my own. "Here, let me help you up."

From this I guessed that I must have fallen. As I got to my feet, he seemed taller and I surmised that I had shrunk by two or three inches. As he'd said, not much of a change at all.

"What happened to the big goblin?" I asked.

"It's the Arrow of Truth, it transforms any being into its true self."

"But he disappeared."

"Didn't you see the huge serpent slink back into the shadows?"

Mercifully, I had not, I'd been too preoccupied watching a missile speeding back towards me. Then I had an idea. I picked up the Arrow from the stone floor and walked to the sad figure seated on the throne.

"If this turns bad, forgive me."

And with that, I pushed the arrowhead sharply into Al's chest. I thought that like me he might shrink some and be able to slip out of the chains. Instead, with the sound of air escaping from a huge tyre, he let out a gasp and like the Goblin King he disappeared. But this time I knew what to expect - sort of. So I carefully picked up the tiny, bedraggled sparrow that now lay motionless upon the throne. I was relieved to feel its heat in my cupped hands, a faint heartbeat and perhaps even the smallest trembling of its wings.

"Come on," said Manro. "The King is not the worst of it. Let's get out while we can."

VI

Cradling the trembling bird in the shelter of my hands, I began to make my way in pitch darkness, upwards through the tunnel. This proved tricky, so I got Manro to remove my hat, which I hoped would provide suitable protection for Al. I still used two hands to carry the improvised nest but knew that if I stumbled it was less likely to further injure the poor thing. Luckily, I needn't have worried as we were soon emerging into a world of flooding light in which the sun was staging a spectacular setting. For a moment, I wondered at the beauty of our world. You've all seen sunsets. You may even have seen some like this, where warm southerly winds have brought sand from the Sahara into our Northern skies to provide reflective prisms which throw colours like jewels across the horizon. I gasped and wanted to share the moment with Al, but the little bird's eyes were closed.

"He's letting the beauty soak into him," said Manro, "We should get him home. He's very much on the edge." The sparrow looked perfectly comfortable in the centre of my soft, brown beanie hat, but its breathing seemed laboured.

"Come on," I said, "I'm sure the Queen will be able to do something."

"I'm not going back," said Manro. "I'm staying here."

"But it's getting dark."

I remembered that it had been the dead of night when we went into that dreadful cavern. How could it be getting dark now?

"It's not just humans that shrink," said Manro. "Time is also compressed in the Faerie realms. I myself have only been there a few weeks, but it feels like an eternity."

"When did you first arrive there?"

"Jan 29th," he answered. "I know because it was just four days before the funeral of our late, great Queen and I'd very much wanted to pay my respects."

I was confused. Then I realised he was talking about the death of Queen Victoria over a hundred years ago. I almost blurted something out to this effect, but realised what a shock that might be for him. Everyone he had known would be long dead. His home, friends, job, all gone. How on earth was he going to cope in the modern world?

"You have to come back... They're expecting us." I realised too late how lame this sounded.

"No, lad or lassie," he said, "It's no place for me. My mind's made up." He seemed rooted to the spot.

"But we have to get Al back."

"You can manage that wee thing alone."

"But the cudgel, the shield, the Arrow.... and what if I fail?" In truth, I was a little scared to go back without him. Would they be angry with me for not forcing Manro to return? Or for stabbing Al? What if he didn't survive? I'd never meant to hurt him. My thoughts were once again an open book.

"Nonsense lad. You did what had to be done. You saved him."

Then I pictured a great celebration with me the hero at the centre of it all. Eating, drinking, the singing of victory songs.

"Whatever you do, don't eat or drink anything," he urged. "Promise me that and in return I'll help you by carrying the weapons to the door."

On the way, Manro explained that Faerie favours were enchanted. To eat or drink anything in that realm renders a human incapable of leaving unless the Queen herself lifts the spell. I was ravenously hungry and didn't know if I had the willpower to resist the full-on glamour of a Faerie feast.

"Stay here with me then."

Although it appeared that once again Manro could read my mind, I tried to hide the pity I felt at his ignorance of how much time had really passed since his first descent. But he turned the tables on me.

"And how much do you think you've lost?"

The hollow under the great tree once again opened at our approach. But as we prepared to enter it, his question found echoes in my imagination. Were my friends and parents still alive? Had I missed my end of term exams? Things couldn't have moved so fast up there, could they? No, surely I'd only been down here a day or two at most. As we walked further into the darkness, my head started spinning. I felt hot. And then cold. I had to remind myself to breathe. My chest hurt and my heartbeat was irregular.

"I have to sit down a moment." By now we'd reached the door.

"What's happening?" he asked.

"I think it's a panic attack."

"It's alright," he said, "we've left them back there. We gave them such a trouncing they'll not return for a while." He had looked about him for goblins before understanding that the attack I spoke of was completely within my own body. So many things in the modern world that Manro had never dreamt of, even the language would catch him out.

"OK," I said, "I'll come back into the realm of humans with you." It tore at me to say this because Al looked so helpless lying there. "But we can't just drop him off and run, can we?"

"No, don't drop him! Here let me."

With a tenderness I'd not seen in him before, Manro took the beanie from me and placed it delicately in front of the door. Turning and seeing that it still held some iridescence from the sunset, he approached the shield and lowered Al into its warm light. Carefully, Manro put the point of the Arrow into one of the tree roots which magically grew, weaving itself into a nest big enough to hold and protect both shield and sparrow. Lifting Aaron's mighty cudgel, he struck the door with such force that I feared it might break. But it held fast. Before the thunderous sound of his striking had finished ringing in the air about us, I heard him shout, "Run lad, run!" and I did.

VII

There was probably a dawn chorus going on. There must recently have been a sunrise. But I only think that now because I remember it was the cold morning dew nipping at my bare feet that led me to search for my shoes. I was trying to look thoroughly all around the base of the tree, but Manro was already off, so I followed. However briefly I'd been underground, I knew in my heart that the Doc Martens would be long gone. I loved those boots. Why on earth had I taken them off in the first place? Ah yes, the Queen. My bag too was lost.

"Do you even know where you're going?" I shouted after Manro. But I was now running to catch up with him.

"Of course, I've seen this park more often than you've had hot ..." He stopped mid-sentence. The university library had come into view and Manro stood looking at it open-mouthed. It was a five-storey building of such modern design and construction that it must have seemed completely alien to nineteenth century experience. To him the concrete pillars and large expanse of glass would defy all the accepted laws of architectural possibility. I

51

thought it very elegant. "Who built this... this monstrosity here?"

I left his question hanging in the air, wondering what he would make of the tower blocks that we were now heading rapidly towards. As the tallest brick-built structures in Europe, at least he might understand enough to appreciate the achievement that they represented.

"Why? Why?" he kept muttering. "Why?"

"Students need somewhere to live," I explained.

"Students?"

Of course, in his time, Wivenhoe House and its surrounding estate would doubtless have been the country residence of some wealthy entrepreneur or aristocratic family. Now it housed the attendant accommodation, lecture halls and facilities of a modern university. At which I confess I had made somewhat lack-lustre academic progress.

It was a misty morning in what the trees considered to be Autumn. I was hoping early Autumn, which would mean that the student-body hadn't yet returned from the long summer vacation. We hadn't seen anyone about, but as most classes didn't start till ten and it was obviously earlier than that, this proved nothing. I had a room on the ground floor of the nearest tower block which I planned to approach from across the lawn, since I remembered leaving the window open. But it was now closed. Familiar brown striped curtains were identically pulled across every window on this, the east facing side of the building. I had hoped to get a glimpse into my room but could see nothing despite pressing my face up to the glass and peering hard where there should have been a gap between the curtains. Manro was intrigued by me standing and staring so intently.

"Is there a magic password?" he asked

"Shhh," I answered instinctively, "I don't want to get mistaken for a peeping Tom."

"What does he have to do with it?"

"Shhh!" again, and I ushered him away. I told him that the entrance was on the far side of the building.

On the way around to the front of the tower block, I explained that the main doors are unlockable. They only give access to the lifts, to the stairwell and to the locked door of the flats at ground level. I thanked my lucky stars for accommodation on the ground floor, in the first year I had a room twelve storeys up. What Manro would have made of the lift-ride didn't bear thinking about.

"Then stop thinking about it!" he shouted. He looked decidedly queasy.

At first, I thought the door to the flats locked, but a firm push proved this was not the case. Students returning late at night often left the lobby door off the latch for drunken friends who hadn't made it back yet. Hence there had been a spate of thefts from the shared kitchen, mainly from fridges. I looked at my companion.

"Wait here," I said.

Manro's clothes were something of an antique even before he'd spent decades underground. We'd recently beaten through gorse and goblins and Manro had at the best of times an uncompromising demeanour. I didn't think he would pass for even a mature student after a rough night out.

I went through the lounge into a corridor of numbered rooms and approached my own. Instinctively I felt in my pocket. Of course! I still had my keys. As I thought about letting myself into the room my hand hesitated at the lock. The fear of alarm, questions, and if I answered these at all truthfully, the inevitable doubts about my sanity, held me back. So instead I knocked, but very quietly. If the occupant was asleep, I didn't want to wake him up. I knew it would be a *him* because the floors of the tower block alternated male and female. At least I wouldn't be mistaken for a predator of some kind. The door opened slightly, and I could see a bleary eye struggling to do the same.

"Yeah. What you doing? Do I know you?"

"Well no, I don't think so, but my name's Robyn. I had this room last year."

He looked at me – incredulous.

"Last year? Are you sure?"

"Or the year before."

I realised how strange such uncertainty must sound, but before I could apologise, he grew hostile.

"Look love, I don't know what you're selling or pushing, more like, but either way jog on. I'm not buying it. This is a boys' dorm; it always has been." He shut the door on me. I raised my hand

and felt the contour of my face. There was not a hint of stubble and it felt ever so slightly … different.

Different! I looked completely different. Manro said that I had hardly changed at all. But I simply had to disagree. For I could see my reflection in the mirror of a communal bathroom directly across the corridor.

"Liar!" I barked at him as I re-entered the lobby. "How could you? How could you lie to me like that?"

"Steady on miss," he said, "I did it for your own good. We *were* in a bit of a pickle at the time. I'm really sorry." With that it all got too much, I guess. I just threw my arms around him and wept. Somehow, he managed to steer me to a low wall outside the building before anyone could come out to investigate the noise. He still had his arm around me as he sat me down.

"It's not so bad, lassie."

Had he called me lassie once before?

"Aye," he said, "just before we took Al back. I thought you might have guessed then. Just think what it's like for Al, transformed into a sparrow. Or the Goblin King. Now he's a great big black serpent. Compared with *them* you've hardly changed at all."

"So am I like this forever?" I asked. "And how? I mean why?"

"The Arrow of Truth is a mystery. I don't know if its effects are permanent. They say no-one's dared to use it for hundreds of years. It does tend to work both ways." He chuckled. "I think you look better now anyway."

I gave him an old-fashioned look.

"Oh no. I'm a happily married man with weans and all. I just meant that you seem to fit better into your skin now, to act more confident. You're more at one with yourself."

I thought about how the Arrow changes things into their true form. Had I always been like this inside? I'd never really fitted in; bullied, left out of games, always a bit of an outsider.

"Come on," he said, "we'd better get you some lasses' clothes or people will stare." The thought of girls' clothes horrified me. I looked down at what I was wearing; a loose, collarless grandad shirt, drainpipe jeans, and bare feet. All very acceptable for a male or a female student around campus. If we were going to travel any distance though I'd have to find some shoes.

"We've plenty of time," said Manro, "to purchase more fitting apparel for a lady."

I was starting to lose patience with Manro. If I'd had my Doc Martens on, I think I would have kicked him. I knew the Students' Union housed a lost property box outside the welfare office. Unclaimed items were placed there after a month or so, for anyone who wanted them.

"Come on," I said to Manro. I was hoping to find shoes but then I had a thought, perhaps the coffee bar would be open. I had no watch to check the time, but it was on the way, and I was starving. I felt in my back pocket and my wallet was still there. I only had a few quid but that would buy us both breakfast.

"Ah, porridge," murmured Manro, "hot, salty oats."

"I don't think they do porridge." I was sure they didn't. "But I can get us both toast, tea and probably some marmalade."

"No porridge? You can keep your marmalade. There's still such a thing as butter, I suppose?"

We walked past a shining hexagonal structure of concrete and glass, the student refectory which wouldn't be open till lunch. I suppose it doesn't look much from the outside. It goes by the name of The Hexagon restaurant or Hex for short.

Dominating the central courtyard of Essex University is a sculpture. I think you'd call it that, or maybe a fountain. It is set in an enormous pool surrounded by a low wall. A painted blue base shows through the clear water, which is about nine inches deep. The 'sculpture' consists of several large buckets, hanging within a spiral tubular frame. Each is of a single bright colour: red, green, blue and yellow, and one is orange too, I think. The largest is at the bottom. As you watch, the water pouring into the top bucket makes it topple once full, disgorging its contents into the lower, slightly larger bucket. If this provides sufficient water for it to reach a tipping point it empties into the one beneath. Every five minutes or so, a domino effect is seen. The top bucket tips and each of the lower vessels follows suit until the one at the bottom relieves itself into the water below, with a resounding splash. It is somehow very satisfying. The coffee bar hadn't opened yet, and I'd spent a happy quarter of an hour observing Manro as he watched the strangely compelling installation. He looked puzzled and I had assumed that, like me on my first arrival in the square two or three years ago, he'd been trying to guess which turn of the top bucket would result in a full cascade.

"It's wonderful," he said at last, "what does it do?"

"It…" I struggled. "It's art," I said. He laughed and almost slapped me on my back before remembering my newly acquired femininity.

"I'm sorry lass, but I think you're pulling my leg. This is engineering. It must power something, or somehow treat the water. It must have a function, surely?"

Now it was my turn to laugh. I'd never really considered the absurdity of so much energy, space and clean drinking water being put into such a fanciful piece of nonsense. In some ways this made it all the more beautiful.

"It's just a bit of fun," I said, and we both laughed.

The two people inside the coffee bar had been busy setting up for the day. Now one of them began unlocking the entrances at either end of the café.

"Breakfast is served, my lord," I joked.

"After you, milady," said Manro, bowing low.

I smiled at that, but I wasn't so keen on him racing past to open the door for me. He was, however, finding it surprisingly heavy.

"Do you need a hand?" I asked and pushed the door he'd been trying to pull.

Being the first in meant there was no queue, so I picked up a brown plastic tray and walked to the waiting barista.

"Can I help you, love?" A few hours ago, he would have said mate, or just asked, "What do you want?" I could feel an interest or curiosity with which I was completely unfamiliar.

"A coffee please. Yes," I carried on, "I'd love a coffee."

"Late night, was it?"

The young man looked quizzically at my companion. "This is your *dad,* right? Tell me he's your dad?" I knew what he was really asking, and it made me angry. I was also finding his attention unsettling.

"Yes," I lied, "he's come to take me home."

I hadn't thought of home. How could I explain things to Mum and Dad? Would they still be in Yorkshire? Together? Alive? Come on now, Robyn, I assured myself, it's only been a year or two at the most, they were together for twenty-three before you... before you what? Disappeared? Went missing? Were last heard of. I looked back at Manro expecting I would have to explain why I'd pretended he was my father. Tears were running down his face. I thought I'd better order for him; "Do you have such a thing as a pot of tea?"

I thought Manro would be more familiar with it being served in a teapot. I should have known this was a ridiculous request. The young guy laughed, and Manro started to sob. I'd forgotten he could read my thoughts; my thinking of home and family must have been so painful to him. For the first time I was glad I couldn't read his.

"Just mugs," said the barista leaning forward. And then, "Is *he* alright?"

"We've had a shock." I said it with deliberate, slow, finality. "Right," I continued, "one mug of tea, one coffee, and two rounds of toast. Each."

"Next please."

The young female assistant had already started making our drinks after deftly dropping four slices of bread into the toaster. While her workmate took my money, she began to serve the next person in the growing queue behind. People were staring.

"Come on, Dad," I said, loud enough for all to hear, "Let's get a seat by the window." I took the tray which now held two steaming mugs: grabbed knives, spoons, sugar, butter, plastic milk pots and marmalade. I snatched the toast and picked up two, no three, napkins. I handed one of those to Manro who looked at me as if I was expecting him to make a paper aeroplane. I made a motion indicating his eyes and he dabbed dutifully at the tears running down his face.

"Dad?" he asked. "I don't think I can get used to that."

"Well, I can't keep calling you "Manro."

"It's Angus," he held out his hand. "Reverend Angus M*u*nro, at your service, madam." The people nearest to us were giggling.

"We're in a play." Lie upon lie! "We're practising for a play."

"Look, Angus. you can see the fountain from here."

The sight of the buckets gleaming as the sunshine inched across the courtyard would, I hoped, cheer him up.

"It's gone," he said at last. "I'm not stupid. I don't know what year it is, but I can read the signs. Everything's so different. My home is gone."

"You don't know that. Look at Wivenhoe House, that's much, much older than you, but it's still standing."

"Aye," he said, "maybe the vicarage will be there, but my friends, my wife, my lovely young boy… They'll all be long gone." I put my hand on his, determined more than ever to find out if my own family were okay.

"Have some toast, Angus."

He stared at the impossibly square slices of toast, then at the plastic tubs of butter, and finally up at me. Once I'd buttered all four slices, I cut them in half and pushed Angus's plate towards him. I added sugar and long-life milk to my drink and dunked a triangle of toast into the hot sweet liquid. I could tell by his expression that, having copied me exactly, he was less than overly impressed.

The campus courtyard was gradually awakening. Students were crossing it on their way to the Lecture Theatre, or going into one of three corners that gave access to the various departments. More than a few just sat on the low wall around the fountain as if expecting the arrival of friends, real or imaginary. There were one or two waiting for Barclays to open, skint after a night of overspend. The bank was to be our next port of call. After breakfast, I'd taken stock of the contents of my pockets: a set of keys to a room I was no longer entitled to enter, NUS, library and rail cards, four pounds fifty-seven pence and my cheque card. I studied the mugshots on the NUS and rail cards. These, I thought, should be enough to prove my identity to the cashier. But did I look like my picture?

"Don't be daft, lass, you've not changed at all, from the neck up you look just the same."

Angus was right. I felt very different indeed, but most students enjoyed a state of flux as they changed hair, style of clothing, or even amongst the more rebellious, got piercings or tattoos. My own similarity to the image on the identity cards would almost certainly be sufficient. I was lucky that my parents had christened me Robyn instead of Mark or Adam.

"Robin's a boy's name," said Angus, "you'd best deepen your voice."

He had a point. There was no telling if one of the cashiers had dealt with me in the past, or what information might be on my records. After all, I'd been missing for two years. I decided to practise.

"Pass me the sugar."

Angus spat out a mouthful of tea.

"No lass, try deepening your voice in a way that doesn't say look at me I can deepen my voice." We both laughed. The bank was open now and I didn't want my confidence to wane further. We strode with purpose across the busy courtyard. Although I hated doing it, I had to ask Angus to wait outside again. This time it wasn't so much his appearance as the fact that I needed to keep myself focused on the task in hand.

"I'd like to make a withdrawal," I said to the cashier and handed her my card.

"So you're Robyn Givens?"

"Yes."

"I'll have to ask you some security questions." When asked, I trotted out my home address, date of birth and mother's maiden name. The cashier looked up.

"How much would you like?"

"Can I have two hundred pounds? I need to take a train home."

She looked at me suspiciously.

"I'm dropping out."

The fact that this was, in effect, the unfortunate reality of the situation hadn't dawned on me till this moment.

"Oh, I'm sorry, love. Of course you can have two hundred pounds, but it will only leave this much in the account." The balance slip showed that my estimate of the maximum funds available had been pretty accurate. "Do you have any cheques in the pipeline?" Her tone was kind. "They could bounce, and even if they don't, an unplanned overdraft is very expensive."

I assured her I didn't.

"Did it *work*?" asked Angus in a voice that betrayed little expectation of my success.

"Oh yes, we now have two hundred and four pounds and fifty-seven pence."

"Two hundred!" he was aghast. "Would you like me to hang onto it for safekeeping?"

"I'm quite capable of looking after my own money," patting my pocket to make sure the envelope was still there. "Come on, we need, ... I need to make a phone call."

Studying Angus's facial expression through little squares of glass held in a grid of bright red metal, was making me chuckle. He couldn't have looked more amazed if I'd got into the phone box and beamed up to a spaceship. Well, not much more amazed anyway. I'd thought about inviting him in, but his presence outside would prevent anyone else coming along and tapping impatiently on the glass. I put a few coins into the phone and stacked the rest on top of the coin-box. Dialling the number took a while, but it was barely enough time for me to compose myself to speak.

"Hi, Mum," I said. "It's me, Robyn."

"Terry, get here. It's Robyn!" I could hear Dad's voice in the background.

"Yes, Terry, I'm sure it is. I know my own son's voice."

"It's alright, Mum. Calm down."

"I'll give you calm down! Where have you been? We've been worried sick. Your poor father! The police! The University! Why haven't you been in touch?" This wasn't going the way I'd imagined.

"It's a long story. I'll tell you all about it when I get home."

"He's coming home, Terry. Yes, he must be alright. He's coming home. No, he doesn't need money. Robyn, do you need money?"

"No, I don't need money, Mum. Hi, Dad!" I shouted, hoping he'd hear. "Look, Mum, I don't know the times of the trains yet. I'll be there sometime this evening."

A young lady had arrived at the telephone box and was having what appeared to be a heated discussion with Angus.

"Oh, and I'm bringing a friend."

I was very relieved to hear the pips go. I had more money that I could have fed in before we were cut off, but I couldn't face answering further interrogation from Mum or handle talking to Dad just yet. After replacing the receiver, I turned and pushed open the heavy door.

"Is this sexist pig really with you?" The crazy-coloured punk hair was pink and blue.

Yes, I'm sorry," I said, "he has Alzheimer's."

"You ought to keep him on a lead then," said the hair, "he's dangerous." With that she entered the box and the door closed behind her.

"What on earth did you say?"

"I only asked who'd done that to her. Then I offered to give him a good hiding on her behalf. Did you see it? Her hair was cut to Bedlam and coloured to match."

"Just don't start conversations with strangers," I suggested. "Not till you've got the hang of the place. And keep any answers short. Minimal. Especially when you meet my mother."

When I'd finished explaining "fashion" to Angus, he agreed that my plan was a good one. He'd thought two hundred pounds was an absolute fortune, several year's wages in fact. I told him that if we found a respectable inn for the night as he was suggesting, then by the time we'd bought train tickets and paid for our meals, we'd be skint. It did take some explaining. I was having an even harder time heading off Angus's desire to visit his own home. We talked as we made a beeline for the student union welfare office. How terrible it would be for him to see his house now occupied by complete strangers. That's if it was still standing. I just couldn't see the point.

"I need to know, Robyn. I need to see it for myself."

VIII

In the box of lost property I found a pair of brightly coloured baseball boots. Green at the front, red at the back and a tongue of bright yellow. At first, I'd thought they would be too small, but I was now a size six and they fitted perfectly.

"You're not listening, Robyn. I need to see for myself."

I could tell his mind was made up, so I steeled myself for whatever emotional maelstrom lay ahead and said, a lot more cheerfully than I actually felt, "Okay, so exactly where are we going?"

It was a desultory walk into Colchester. On more than one occasion I had to stop Angus accidently stepping into traffic. He cared so much about what lay ahead that the here and now seemed to have lost all reality to him. We walked in silence and anyone observing us would surely have thought him mad. He was sometimes muttering to himself, sometimes stopping and looking about him like a startled animal, and always with a deep frown and grimly set jaw that told of inner turmoil. As we rounded the corner, his church came into sight and for a moment he seemed to perk up and actually appeared noticeably taller. I hoped he wouldn't see the prominent noticeboard announcing the church's new identity as a craft market and café. Angus's face was going through a remarkable series of emotions, joy, pain, sorrow and finally guilt.

"What do you have to feel guilty about?" I asked. He looked shocked.

"Can you read my mind now, lassie?"

I was glad I couldn't. The realisations that must be weighing on him, the finality, the grief. I stretched out my hand in an offer to take his.

"No," he said grimly, "I can deal with this. The parsonage is through the churchyard."

I followed him through the creaking iron gate and around the side of the great stone temple of St. Mary at the Wall. The noonday sun was casting autumnal shadows onto recently cut grass. Trees were still holding onto most of their summer colour but here and there russet and golden leaves lay softly on the ground. Some had even encroached onto the otherwise immaculate rectangles of stone which marked the final resting place of many faithful souls.

When I saw Angus fall to his knees, I instinctively rushed to his side. I put my hand under one arm to help him to his feet. Then I saw what had caused him to collapse. At the side of the building engraved in stone:

> **HERE LIES**
> **ANGUS MUNRO**
> **PASTOR OF THIS PARISH.**
> **DECEASED JUNE 12TH**
> **1937.**

I was struck dumb.

After a while I found my voice; "How on earth…."

"It's alright, Robyn. I'm no ghost. It shocked me too at first. But this isn't my resting place. It's that of my wee boy Angus." He wept then. As I held his limp hand, I cried too, from the pit of my stomach. He managed to gather himself before I could and came to my assistance. "Help me if you can, lassie. I've been down on these old knees for too long."

We would have seemed a sorry sight as we left the shadow-pooled garden of remembrance. He hadn't wanted to go any further towards the vicarage.

"I couldn't bear to see what they've done to my garden." I thought Angus might once more have trouble holding it all together and I looked around for somewhere to sit. "No," he assured me, "exercise will help. Let's press on."

Thankfully, as we walked from the church to the railway station something of his vigour returned, and by the time we saw its white picket fencing, he seemed quite twitchy.

"I must confess to being a bit of a train spotter," he said, "I only wish I had my little book to jot down the engine numbers." We purchased tickets and sat on the platform for London-bound passengers.

"The next train at platform one will be the 12:37 to London Liverpool Street." The tannoy announcement almost made Angus jump out of his seat. Then he laughed at the sound of the approaching engine, this at least would be something familiar. After he'd recovered from the disappointment of it not being a steam locomotive, Angus appeared to enjoy boarding the train, hearing the whistle of the guard, and getting underway. He was startled almost immediately by the disembodied voice announcing the times of stops up to and including Liverpool Street. He soon settled into the steady rhythm of the wheels, however, and I felt it appropriate to smile. The one-hour journey to London passed without me managing to convey to Angus the enormity of the difficulties ahead.

"You mustn't mention Faeries to my mother."

"Why has she had a bad experience with them in the past?"

I would have explained that their very existence would be as nonsensical to her as contemporary fashions were to him, but my fellow traveller was completely distracted. The view through the carriage window changed constantly, revealing buildings, vehicles and machinery the likes of which he'd never even imagined.

"Yes," I said to him. "Sit down. It's just a trac-tor." And so it was that I found myself explaining the names, uses and even the origins of the trap-pings of modern life.

"It's called a Walkman," I whispered loud enough to be heard above the faint noise from a teenager's headphones. "What she's listening to is *music*." After the boarding of so many passengers at Chelmsford, she'd found no other seats free but the one next to me, or to Angus. She glanced at Angus and her shoulder brushed against mine as she sat. I was glad she had the headphones on, or goodness knows what she'd have made of our con-versation.

"What do you mean, you won't lie?" I asked him.

"I am a Christian. I will not forswear myself."

"No, for God's sake don't swear in front of Mum."

"Nor Robyn, will I take the Lord's name in vain."

I apologised for any offence and could see him exercising Christian forgiveness.

"I meant for pity's sake. But you must see that we can't tell the truth."

"Perhaps I can live with that, but I will not tell a lie."

For the last ten minutes of the trip silence sat between us. As the first buildings came into sight, I could sense Angus's growing excitement. Earlier he'd told me how he'd taken the train journey to London on more than one occasion, albeit some ninety years past. I'm not sure how the capital looked now compared to his previous visits, but Angus seemed impressed.

"It's all so clean," he said. "And yet so messy." I think I understood what he meant by that.

"You get yourself ready for a shock." I thought it was good to give plenty of advance warning. "We'll be going underground."

"Surely not, there are no Faerie gates in London, are there?"

When I recovered myself enough to explain, it was my turn to be surprised and just a little embarrassed. He'd actually travelled on The Underground before. He'd even experienced electrically operated lifts and carriages similar to the ones we'd be travelling in. He hadn't, however, seen an escalator until the one we were now standing in front of. Some people were quite rude about his reluctance to step onto it. In the end I had to hold his hand and make a game of it.

"Now, one, two, and on three we take the step." As we approached the "teeth" at the bottom, it was all I could do to stop him turning to climb the steps back to the top. "It's OK," I assured him. "It's just the same, one, two, and then step off."

His initial confusion about what I had meant by The Underground had however given me an idea. The journey from London Euston to Manchester gave me a chance to explain it. But he did take some convincing.

"You can tell your mother what you like," he argued, "but I won't say we met on The Underground. That's quite different to where we did meet."

But I persisted and eventually found a way round his obstinate adherence to the truth. I would refer to The Underground and if he was pressed on this, he could say, "Aye, underground." It took considerable negotiation. Almost the entire two hours to Manchester were taken up with similar preparations. Leaving aside when we'd met, which proved to be a completely intractable sticking point, other details fell into place. I would tell my parents that Angus had been a student of Divinity. I would introduce him as Angus Munro who I'd met at the University, (well, under it actually, but no need to be too pedantic). If the Reverend bit came out it would be easily explicable. What they had to think was that I'd spent the last couple of years living alone in London before bumping into him on "The Underground."

"Aye, underground," he muttered.

We were good but not close friends, and I would tell Mum and Dad that some unfortunate and very recent deaths in his family meant that he had no one in the world to turn to, so I'd invited him to come home with me. I knew that my parents would have too much tact and sympathy to enquire further as to Angus's family or background. How I'd been spending almost two years in London without contacting them would be a different matter. I had sufficient confidence in my ability to spin a lie.

Angus's state of bereavement would hopefully mit-
igate any odd behaviour on his part.

"Will you look at that?" he exclaimed and then
in a loud whisper, "The poor girl's had her ear and
her nose safety-pinned back on again. Couldn't she
afford a surgeon?"

I was learning the art of throwing a disarming
shrug and an indulgent expression towards the re-
cipients of all such observations. I knew I'd need
much more than this to deal with the coming fur-
nace of questions and admonitions from a fully
stoked mother. Crossing Manchester from Piccadil-
ly to Victoria station proved even harder than travel
in London had been. Londoners never look at you.
They've learned not to comment on unconvention-
al behaviour. Up north, speaking and friendliness
go hand in hand.

"He's a bloody bam pot. Should be locked up."

The sentiments, if not these exact words, were a
common response to my explanations of Angus's
helpful suggestions and impertinent curiosity.
Eventually, we reached Victoria station and the
comparative safety of a very old-fashioned train.
Each carriage had several small compartments with

a manual sliding door that granted or barred access to the windowed corridor alongside.

"This is more like it," said Angus as he settled into the upholstery and fell soundly asleep. I envied him.

I woke him up five minutes before we were due to arrive in Todmorden, and he berated me for allowing him to slumber. The fact that he had been sleeping so soundly that even the attentions of the ticket collector didn't wake him, made me feel he was being unfair. Anyway, he hadn't missed much. The ten-minute walk from the railway station to my parent's house was taken up with rehearsing our agreed "truth".

"My God, Robyn," said Mum, "you look terrible." She threw her arms around me so fiercely that I was quite taken aback. I'd seen her just three weeks previously, but for her (and I had to remind myself of this), it had been more than two years.

"Let me take a look at you," and then stepping back, "you've lost so much weight. Have you eaten today? You're not on drugs, are you?"

Drugs. That was one of my mother's greatest fears. Heroes of her youth like Judy Garland and

Marilyn Monroe had fallen under their evil influence. She'd never encountered "drugs" personally but felt such close kinship to these screen idols that their wasted potential had devastated her. It hadn't helped that the welcome pack sent by the university had included a Students' Union handbook with details of the Legalise Cannabis Society and a number for the Drugs Helpline.

"No Mum, I'm not on drugs. This is Angus."

"Angus Munro at your service."

As I'd instructed, he held out a hand as if to shake hers. No one had ever, to my knowledge, kissed my mother's hand. She looked at his extended hand uncertainly, stared into his face, and asked somewhat icily,

"So how do you two know each other?"

"Where's Dad?" I asked.

"He's popped out for biscuits. You know what he's like." I knew Dad had a sweet tooth and our imminent arrival would have given him an excuse to circumvent Mum's tough-love approach to his diet.

"Robyn!" I heard Dad's voice. Turning, I saw the carrier bag swing around me so it wouldn't be crushed between us.

"Come on you lot inside - what will the neighbours think? And watch those biscuits, Graham. They're probably all broken now."

"Crumbs," said Dad playfully and we laughed precisely because we'd heard the joke so often before. I'm not sure Angus got it, but he laughed anyway, somewhat awkwardly. "You've no coats then? You're lucky it's still mild. And where are your bags? What the devil's been going on, Robyn?"

"I left my coat underground," said Angus.

Again, Mum eyed him suspiciously.

"That's right Mum. We had to travel across London on the underground in the rush hour and someone stole our bags." I could see Angus flinching. This wasn't one of our agreed "truths". Fortunately Dad bought it.

"Folk are so wicked," he said.

"Never mind. You got here. That's all that matters. I'm sure some of your Dad's things will fit your new friend and you left most of your old clothes in your room."

"Can I go up to my room now Mum? I can show Angus the toilet."

"I'm sure he's seen a toilet before." Angus was now blushing.

"Of course. You'll both want to clean up before supper. I've made a pie. I wasn't sure what time you'd get here so I just have to stick it in the oven." Mum's cheese and potato pie, Angus was in for a treat.

"Come on," I said to him, "I'll show you where things are."

My room hadn't changed at all. There were a lot of letters on the bed though. I think Mum must have put them there as a silent rebuke. Most were from the university; some were from the local authority. Those marked urgent had been opened. I knew there was nothing that couldn't wait.

"I'll show you the bathroom," I said.

Once he had gotten used to the "lever operated flushing mechanism," learnt where everything was, and been shown how to lock and unlock the door, I left Angus to it. I went into the room I'd had since childhood, sat on the edge of the divan and broke into tears. That's how Mum found me, head in my hands and rocking back and forth.

"Oh, Robyn, come on now. What will your friend think?" She paused and my sobbing stopped. "He seems nice, you *are* just…"

"No," I blurted, "we're just friends, close friends." Then I remembered the rehearsed truth; "But not too close. He's recently bereaved. Lost his whole family in a dreadful accident. He has no-one."

"Oh, the poor love. How terrible. But where have you been Robyn? And why haven't you been in touch?"

"Can we talk tomorrow, Mum? I'm so tired right now," I could smell the pie as it cooked downstairs, "and starving!"

"What is that delicious aroma?" said Angus. "Have we died and awoken in heaven's kitchen?" Mum laughed.

"He's as daft as you. I can see why the two of you get along. Give me ten minutes then come down to the living room for your tea."

To Mum, the words dinner, tea and supper were pretty interchangeable. But it was a world in which the term "lunch" was never heard - that was always referred to as "yer dinner."

"Dinner is served," she shouted theatrically from downstairs. It was now nearly ten o'clock at night and I relaxed in the knowledge that there would be no questions while we ate. It would be easy enough to feign tiredness afterwards. In the event, pretence wasn't needed. By eleven o'clock Angus and I were both tucked up in bed; me under a Star Trek duvet and Angus in a feather-filled sleeping bag on my bedroom floor.

A few weeks later, Mum was getting along famously with Angus. Unfortunately, much of their fun was at my expense.

"Oh, he's like that with you too, is he?"

"Yes," Angus answered, "very economical with the truth."

"So you're not a mature student?"

"No he just said that because he's embarrassed about me being a vicar."

"The daft ha'p'orth. Sometimes I think he doesn't know me at all."

"I think he doesn't really know himself."

"Well I'm glad there's someone sensible in his life for once." Mum inspected the egg-whites Angus had been beating in preparation for one of her deliciously light meringues.

"Oh Angus, you've definitely got the knack." Then she passed him the spoon which she'd been using to mix the lemon filling. He dutifully licked it and handed it back. It was as if I wasn't there. I can't say that I felt entirely comfortable with this growing confederacy. Up till now, I'd managed to conceal my change of gender by not trying too obviously to conceal it; no deepening of the voice, no hearty back-slapping, no pretending to suddenly like football or be interested in motor cars. In fact, Angus's enthusiasm for both made him a natural ally for my father. Perhaps if my parents hadn't been quite so intrigued by their new guest, they might have noticed more of a change in me. Perhaps not, for what Angus had said still rang true; I hadn't really changed much at all. But I had changed sex and in some ways, this made sharing a room with Angus difficult. We developed a habit of always knocking before entering, and I also found it better to dress before leaving the bathroom. As I walked around the house, a towel round my waist was no longer sufficient to protect my dignity, or my secret. Most of my old clothing was both loose fitting and unisex, and anything that wasn't I simply didn't wear. Angus took to current fashion like a cat to water, but despite a few nasty experiences with the zipper, he became an enthusiastic convert.

"A shirt with the collar attached is so much easier, Robyn. I don't know why you insist on wearing those collarless things." Grandad shirts were fashionable, but that wasn't the whole of it. I now found collared shirts just a little bit "manly".

One morning while we were sitting together in his shed, Dad and I almost had a conversation.

"Is anything wrong?" he'd asked. "Is there anything I should know about?"

"No," I lied, and then more truthfully, "I've never been happier."

The weeks quickened into months. I'd signed on and was receiving unemployment benefit. Angus couldn't believe how quickly we'd squandered the fortune I'd withdrawn in Colchester. He would have looked for a job, but with no national insurance number and a somewhat complicated history, this avenue was closed to him. For now, he seemed content to help Mum about the house and Dad in the garden when "Graham," as he insisted Angus should call him, wasn't at work.

"Graham does work hard," he remonstrated, "you should give him a break." I kept my temper. And I wasn't idle. I had the letters to the local authority and to the university to write. Explanations as to why I hadn't finished my second year proved harder to contrive than the reasons for my inability to repay any of the maintenance grant. But both bodies seemed happier once I'd expressed my intention to complete my course of study after the summer. Until then we had the walks. Angus hadn't seen Yorkshire before, so showing him The Blackrock, Eagle's Crag and the eerie beauty of the Bridestones was a pure and unsolicited delight. He had however, heard of Stoodley Pike. He knew that the original monument, raised to commemorate the peace that followed Napoleon's defeat, had fallen on the eve of the Crimean War. The result of a lightning strike. The national press at that time were running with the war as their lead story. So even a nine-year-old boy living in Colchester didn't escape the buzz caused by such a coincidence. In fact, many saw the great Colchester earthquake of 1884, which happened some thirty years after the Stoodley disaster, as a similar portent of doom.

"Can we visit the monument tonight?" asked Angus. "It's a full moon."

I didn't know what the moon had to do with anything, but I agreed, as I wanted to miss a James Bond special that was on T.V. Dad was very excited about the programme, some twenty-first anniversary thing, and I knew we'd get into an argument about Ronnie Reagan. He was due to give a live presidential message and I wouldn't be able to stop myself. I hated that man, and Dad and I had been having too many "words" lately.

"Why did you drop out, Robyn? Why couldn't you stick at it?" Sticking at it was one of Dad's things. He'd stuck at being a machinist all his working life. He'd stuck at looking after his parents and then at renovating their old house. He'd stuck at being married to Mum. "Your Mum and I were so proud of you making it to university. All that opportunity. Wasted!"

"I may go back and finish my degree, Dad. I've written to admissions."

"But why give up like that? Why?"

"I met a woman."

Dad smiled broadly. "I knew it. I told your Mum she needn't worry on that score. Where's this girl now? Did it end badly?"

"In a way, Dad. I never got to say goodbye."

It was a bit of a stretch to refer to the Queen of the Faeries as a woman. I'd got used to stretching the truth.

"Perhaps it's not really over then. But you should finish your studies first. You only get one crack at life."

I knew it was over though. I'd never get to see her again. As I remembered the power of her glamour, a part of me was glad.

The four of us sat down to supper later than our usual time of six o'clock. It being a Friday, there was fish and chips that we ate out of newspaper. Dad got his pay packet on a Friday; Mum got a night off from cooking and washing dishes. With both of them being in a good mood, I felt I could be truthful.

"Angus and I are going to walk up to the Pike."

"That's a nice idea. I'll make you a packed lunch."

"No Mum, we're going tonight."

"Don't be daft," said Dad, "you'll miss that show with Thora Hird. You love that, and there's the Octopussy special."

"I'm not really into James Bond anymore. It's kids' stuff."

"Well, the President of the USA doesn't agree. So there! Smarty pants."

"I don't see," said Mum in a voice that said there'd be no more bickering, "why you don't leave off going till the morning."

"I want to see it under a full moon Mrs. Givens. I've heard it's spectacular."

"Well if that's what you want Angus and it's not one of Robyn's crazy ideas, that's different. Wrap up warm though. It'll be dark soon so take a torch and be careful."

We set off just before eight, promising not to stay up there too long, and to be back before eleven, Dad's bedtime during the week. He winked as he told me there was no overtime tomorrow, so I knew an early night wasn't set in stone. Stoodley Pike is less than three miles from my parents' house, and I thought it would take an hour to walk each way. There being nothing up there to occupy us for more than about twenty minutes I had felt confident that we could stick to our promise, but now I was regretting having made it.

"Keep up," said Angus. "We mustn't worry your mother unduly."

Although older than me by some twenty years (or one hundred and fourteen depending on how you look at it) Angus was taller and, I'm ashamed to say, considerably fitter. The walk up to the Pike is entirely and steeply uphill, or so it seemed as I kept hurrying to catch up with the dark circle in front of me. The narrow road was lined with trees and all I could see was Dad's broad brimmed hat which Mum had been only too happy to pass on to Angus.

"Angus, slow down," I pleaded, sounding foolish in my breathlessness.

"We're never going to make it back by eleven unless we get a move on, it's been an hour already."

The watch. Another of Dad's bequests.

"Time really doesn't matter, Angus. I need to stop."

He did, and when I caught up with him, he turned me around to look back at what so held his gaze. We had climbed sufficiently high for the upper end of the Calder Valley to be lying spread out beneath us. The orange glow of the streetlights and the illuminated windows of all the little houses looked so cosy. Yet the safety and the welcome which they would offer appeared distant now. Only very occasionally did a car's headlights move through the town, but from up here they did so silently. In fact, there was no sound around us at all.

"Yes," said Angus, "from up here you can forget how much we differ from the Faeries." He was right; it had reminded me of looking into the miniature furnished chambers of the oak tree all those weeks ago.

"Come on," he broke the spell. "If we crack on, we can be there for five and twenty past." I wished that Mum had been able to give him one of those new digital watches.

Before we had quite reached the Pike, something very unsettling happened. We suddenly became aware of dozens of eyes watching us. They were reflected in the moonlight and moved rapidly in and out of the trees. I was petrified until one pair of eyes jumped out in front of me, and I laughed.

"They're only squirrels!" I shouted. But Angus had continued to walk briskly ahead.

One of them, just to my left, bared its teeth and hissed at me. I ran then, but looking behind me while still running, I saw a seething mass scampering after me, all jumping over each other, teeth chattering. When I finally pulled up alongside Angus, he was rooted to the spot. Ahead of him I could see Stoodley Pike, the moon hung in a cloudless sky behind. Bolts of lightning were earthing themselves through the monument into the ground beneath. The squirrels ran either side of us. I was relieved that none were making contact with my feet or ankles, let alone darting up the legs of my flared jeans. They were headed for the Pike, climbing up, down, over, all around the monument as though it was the squirrel equivalent of catnip. I couldn't have gone any closer, the combination of crazed rodents and forked lightning was truly terrifying.

"Be brave," said a voice in my head. I recognised it at once and looked all about me, until I saw perched on a dry-stone wall the nervous silhouette of what I knew to be a small sparrow.

"Al!" I cried. "Angus! It's Al."

Part Three

Stoodley Pike, Calderdale

IX

"I'm not going anywhere near that thing - lightning can be deadly." Angus was arguing with Al even though the bedraggled little creature hadn't uttered a word. It was then that I realised Angus could hear all of Al's thoughts, not just the ones Al chose to share.

"You can't mess with lightning," protested Angus.

"It's not lightning." Al made this a thought for both of us to hear. "Can't you see it's going upward?"

He was right, my brain must have been trying to make sense of the illogical information being sent to it by my eyes. Now that it had been pointed out to me, I could see that each blue flash started in the earth and travelled up the stones of the Pike before arcing into the sky.

"And that's supposed to make us feel safer?" glowered Angus.

"I'm supposed to make you feel safer," said Al. And somehow, he did. I don't know whether it was a Faerie glamour, the calming tone of voice, or the trust I'd placed in Al, but somehow I knew we'd be alright.

"Follow me," he said, and flew towards the Pike. The dark monolith looked enormous as it stood on the crest of the hill before us, though I knew it to be only a hundred and twenty feet high. I hoped Al wasn't going to fly to the upper gallery. Climbing those narrow steps with electricity, of whatever sort, racing about us would test my trust in Al beyond its limits.

"Your poor mother," said Angus, as we walked slowly forwards.

I was relieved to see a tunnel open in front of us that offered up an entrance under the monument, after his lengthy stay in the Faerie world I thought Angus would be less so. Then I had a moment of terrible anxiety. What if we weren't ten or twenty minutes late? What if to those up here, we were down there for days, weeks, months, or once again, for years?

"Don't worry," thought Al alighting on my shoulder, "you'll be home in time for supper."

I'd have found this reassuring if it wasn't for the fact that we'd already had supper some three hours earlier.

"You can't trust 'em," muttered Angus loudly. But he was already walking ahead of us with a grim determination. Al being perched on my shoulder; I had an excuse to walk more hesitantly behind Angus as I saw him descend into impenetrable darkness.

"Careful lassie there's something metallic here."

"Angus?" I needed to hear his voice again as my eyes hadn't been able to make out anything in the thick blackness all around.

"Just here," called Angus, and he tapped on the iron to make it ring. I inched forward, hands in front of me, until I felt, at chin height, the cold metal of a tubular rung. This at least gave me something to clutch on to. I could tell by the proximity of his breathing that Angus was the other side of the ladder.

"I hope you're not scared of heights," he said.

"Or the dark," thought Al, and I remembered his very first words to me.

Looking upwards, only the top of the ladder emerged from the darkness, beneath a small circular opening that was letting in moonlight. I guessed it to be about twelve, fifteen, maybe twenty feet up. I wasn't at all sure about the wisdom of climbing to a hole that wasn't big enough for anyone but Al to fit through. Then I had a very discomforting realisation. My feet were getting wet, my ankles, my shins. The chamber was filling with water, and it had already reached my knees. Without thinking we climbed, Angus on one side of the ladder and I on the other. Occasionally our hands, feet, or knees would touch as we grabbed at the rungs and pulled ourselves towards the top. The water was climbing almost as quickly, and Al was starting to panic. That really frightened me. I'd never known him make a sound, but now I heard him chirruping and wittering in alarm as he fluttered back and forth from my shoulders to Angus's, round our heads, and back again. The next time he landed on my companion's shoulder, Angus picked him up with the same hand in which he held his hat, and put the frightened bird on top of his head, and the hat very carefully on top of that. This calmed Al and there was silence, even inside my head. The water, despite our best endeavours to escape, was up to our waists and still rising.

"Take a deep breath and pray," said Angus as it rose to my chest. I could see that he held his hat in place right up until the time the water reached my eyes and instinctively, they closed. I heard a whirring above my head and opened them to see overlapping discs of metal sliding horizontally above me like the aperture of a camera. But whereas a camera's eye opens in a fraction of a second, this seemed to take forever. I'd reached the top of the ladder but had to let go of the rungs altogether to allow my legs to kick me to the surface of the stillness above. As my head broke through the water a desperate lungful of air flooded into my body.

Remembering the others were behind, I swam to the edge of the pool and felt stone, pushed myself onto the bank, and waited for them to appear. Nothing disturbed the reflection of my crouched outline with the full moon behind. After what had to be the worst minute of my life, and the longest, I lowered my head into the water and opened my eyes. I was staring into a cylinder of stone. The ladder was gone, and it was now a perfectly natural barrel of grey and brown boulders. Penetrating daggers of moonlight vied for my attention but there was no other movement. I pulled my face from the water and gasped for air. There was a sound like a distant song, almost lost in the mournful, moorland wind. Perhaps it was Al's thinking that told me to follow that faint voice to its source.

Wet through, I raised myself unsteadily to my feet and ran into the wild buffeting gusts. The clouds moved hungrily across the face of the moon finally swallowing it completely. There was not even a hint of where the light had been. My lungs, already exhausted, were burning with the effort of running towards the voice. How long could I survive like this? Maybe I'd already pushed myself too far. The full moon appeared from behind the clouds, and through the mist I saw them. Rising up out of the earth like ancient sculptures, but completely natural in shape and substance. The Bridestones.

You can see Bridestones Moor from the top of Stoodley Pike, but there are miles of the Calder Valley separating them. To walk from one side of the dale to the other takes a couple of hours of hard hiking; half of it down and then once you cross the River Calder, half uphill. It was obvious to me that I had been transported to the stones by some sort of enchantment. If the forces of magic were involved, then my friends could be anywhere. Close to the Bridestone that looks like a roughly hewn upturned pyramid, I found a place between two enormous outcrops that provided some shelter. I looked at my fingers which were puce and flecked with mud. I couldn't feel them, just the pins and needles which failed to extend to the limits of my hands. There was nothing I could do but drop to my haunches and curl into a tight ball. I tried to make my head disappear further into my jacket, clasping my knees and pulling them into my chest. I sobbed.

"Hey come on lass." As he reached out and held me, I leant into Angus and threw my arms around him.

"She feared we were lost." I'm sure that Al thought this for Angus's benefit, but I too found it comforting. "Look at her, she's had a terrible time of it."

"I do have eyes you know," said Angus, "and a heart. Come on lass, everything's fine now. We must have climbed out before you."

"But how? You were behind me."

"Who can explain any of this? We thought you'd gone ahead, or we'd have waited."

"There's no time for explanations," thought Al. "We've work to do."

Al did however explain some things to me as we walked towards the singing. It was as if a memory just popped into my head and took no time at all. Like me, Angus and Al had emerged from the pool. They too had waited, they too had searched under the water, or at least Angus had. Freed from the hat, Al had become increasingly agitated, beseeching Angus to come with him towards the same mournful voice I had tried to follow. This had been where they were headed when they discovered me in my pitiful hunched up state. Al hadn't intimated pitiful. But as these thoughts, or memories rather, were transferred to me, I was ashamed of just how miserable I had looked. I don't think I would have judged anyone else in that position as harshly as I did myself. From Al I could feel only understanding, compassion and the need to "let it go."

X

As we approached a group of rocks a few hundred yards from the Bridestones proper, I could see a solitary figure sat on the long flat top of a high, rough-sided stone. The legend she sang made me want to drop to my knees and cry once more.

The song told of an enchantress who every full moon would dance in the shape of a white doe. Her joy at doing so almost moved me to tears. Then the tears did come, for a man whose marriage proposal she had rejected set dogs on her. Ordinary dogs she could easily outrun, but these had been joined by an old witch in the shape of a hound. This magical beast was able to catch her and bring her down. The witch, who was in the pay of Lord Towneley, the would-be suitor, explained how he could keep the doe captive. He had to lead the deer to his castle bound only by a silken cord. In the morning the imprisoned animal would resume its true shape;

that of the beautiful Lady Sybil. The most moving part of the lament was how she hated being unable to leave the castle, and bathe in the moonlight:

"Will no-one loose me from this thread,

Must I always be in thrall?

Oh to dance beneath the stars

Lost in all things fancy full."

The last two words echoed into the night like an incantation. She must be the Lady Sybil I thought as we got closer. I could see a golden thread like a ring of light all around her. Sat with her ankles pulled up, she was able to lay her head on her knees: her hands, palms down, on the rock beside her. The face was turned away from us, long hair, like silver, melting down and about her. The binding cord looked easy enough to escape from; it was simply draped over the back of her neck, hanging loosely till it ran over her wrists, before being looped under the soles of her feet.

"Why doesn't she just shake it off?" I asked and felt about as foolish as I ever have in my life. For the others were at the foot of the rock and I was talking to myself. Angus easily climbed the eight feet to the figure on the stone altar, but he struggled to lift the weight of the cord from her ankles, while Al seemed to be using every ounce of his strength to shift the loop encircling her neck.

"Don't just stand there gawping, lass, get up here and lend a hand."

Try as I might, I couldn't follow Angus to the summit. I was still wet, it was dark, and twice I slipped, almost injuring myself in the process.

"Come up the easy way," thought Al kindly, "before you hurt yourself."

The way Angus had climbed was much easier and proved more successful than my vain heroic efforts had been. I'd wasted a lot of energy in a futile attempt to scale the almost sheer east-facing side of the stone. On the opposite face, the one Angus had gone straight to, there were footholds and handholds in exactly the right places. I climbed up and stood looking at Angus.

"What do we do now?" To make myself heard I had to shout into the wind.

"You take hold of the thread at hand and foot to the left of her, I'll do the same on this side." Angus spoke calmly and as his actions were a mirror of what I was meant to do, it would be easy enough to copy him. Al, of course, needed no instruction. He had already flown behind the enchantress' head and was lifting the cord a few inches from her neck. At first it felt like I was trying to prise a vein of precious metal from the rock itself. However, by bending my knees and curving my back I managed to lift my portion of the thread clear. As soon as it was free of her hunched up figure, the ring of gold moved like a cloud's shadow across the dark moor, eventually disappearing over the horizon's edge. At this point it was no bigger than a distant star.

The lady looked up, her eyes moon-full.

"Your Highness," thought Al.

The last time I'd seen her she'd been robed in majesty and protected by her guards. Now, wet, exhausted, dressed only in a tattered shift she still looked every inch a queen. As she rose to her feet, as easily as a cork to the water's surface, there seemed to be a halo of moonlight about her.

"We don't have much time," she began. "The ring will be, even now, returning to the hands of he who forged it. Hush! I will grant each of you a gift as a way of saying thank you. Whatever you decide to ask for, if it lies within my power, you will have it. Mr. Munro - you first"

"I'd like forgiveness Your Majesty." The Queen was taken aback.

"For what?"

"I broke my word. When we left your realm to rescue Al from the goblins, I promised to return." She looked at him with such stern tenderness.

"Step forward, kneel and bow your head." the Queen took out a long, white-bladed knife. With the moon at its height and sky now cloudless, the curved blade was too bright to look at for long. I couldn't look at the handle either because it was as bleak as night is black. Instead I stared into her expressionless face as she reached into Angus' hair and pulled out a single silver thread. Fine as gossamer it shimmered in the moonlight. Cutting it with some effort, she declared, "You are no longer bound to me or to Faerieland."

Tears ran down Angus's face. "But I only asked forgiveness," he said, looking into her eyes.

"That is what you have. Learn to accept it." I helped the poor man to his feet. "And you, Robyn - what do you desire?"

"Could you reverse the enchantment," I struggled at the import of the words, "the enchantment of the Arrow?"

"The Arrow of Truth sings with a timeless voice. However, truth is always delicately balanced. So it is much easier to overturn than a lie. A falsehood gains strength with every repetition. Truth can be altered, hidden, *man*ipulated. But that is not the Faerie way. To reverse such a powerful song is asking me to risk much."

I felt ashamed of the lies and deceit I'd always thought of as harmless ways of getting what I wanted, or evading blame for what I'd done.

"Please, Your Majesty, if you could just…", but her voice cut across mine.

"I haven't finished." Her eyes were fierce in the moonlight, and I was afraid. "Think, Robyn Givens.

Think hard on what you want. Sometimes that's not the easiest thing to see, let alone accept."

"I want this," I proclaimed, "I really, really want this."

"Very well," and the fingers of the Queen traced a crescent across the night arcing brightly like a kaleidoscope of firefly.

I looked down for confirmation. I was still me.

"Robyn," said Al, "what on earth?"

Al stood in front of me, no longer a sparrow. I didn't answer his question. I was so happy to see him again. So glad to have what I'd done, undone, that I pulled him close, and hugged him.

"I hope you don't mind," I blubbed, "you looked quite content to be a bird."

"Thank you," Al said, "for now I can be with my friends."

"Will you be going straight back to them?"

"No need," he said, "you're both already here." At that Angus joined us in our huddle.

"I hate to end such revels," urged the Queen, "but we must all leave before my husband returns."

"Husband?"

"The giant Todmer captured me and bound me to this rock. If you had not freed me before sunrise, here I would have always remained." The Queen looked to the horizon. "Quickly! It comes."

I looked about me expecting to see some lumbering goliath. But all I could see was the first faint light of dawn outlining the horizon. For a moment I thought that this was what the Queen meant and caught a glimpse of an ancient pattern. The interplay of night and death, life and darkness, in which there is no winner, loser, wrong or right, just a never-ending game of shadows chased. Then I felt the earth shaking beneath me, slightly at first. As it intensified, I heard a sound like distant thunder which soon adopted the rhythm of a quickening footfall.

"He knows that I am free - fly! fly!" And she did, up into the gathering dawn, and away.

"I think I can still fly," said Al, "but if you two don't want to be a giant's breakfast, you'd best follow me." With that he ran, and we followed. Back to the deep pool into which each of us dived, submerged, and were gone. It was completely disorientating to feel the air in my body carry me towards what should have been the bottom of the pool. Once more the world had turned topsy-turvy, and I saw light above my head as I came up inside the stone walls of Stoodley Pike. The iron ladder was again rising above us, and I could tell from a patch of blue sky visible through the aperture that it was no longer night. Mum was going to kill me. As I clambered from the water, Angus announced that he'd found a door, which I saw him open.

"Don't worry," said Al, "I told you I'd get you home for supper."

Part Four

The Lightning-struck Tower

XI

I could feel the warm sunshine as I began to follow Angus out. But before I could question Al's promise, Angus grabbed me by the arm.

"Get out, get out quick," he shouted. "The blasted tower is on fire."

Angus and I stood looking up at thick smoke coming from the Pike's summit.

Al was laughing as he sauntered towards us.

"It's not on fire. This is the Pike that collapsed in 1854. It's got a room for sitting in and a fireplace. There's obviously someone up there."

"How is this possible?" said Angus. "What have you done?"

Al explained that his own wish had obviously been granted. He had made it silently in a way that kept it private, even from Angus.

"I wanted it to be a surprise," Al said. "I asked the Queen that you be allowed to see your family again."

"My wife was an infant in 1854," shouted Angus, "I was only a child myself."

"I'm sorry," said Al. "I guess the Queen didn't really understand which family I meant. You could still visit your parents."

"They'd be younger than I am now. What would I say to them?"

Al became deadly earnest. "You're not allowed to speak to anyone here, nor eat anything. Just don't touch anything really. You're only allowed this glimpse of the past as an observer. You can't change anything. You mustn't."

"I guess Todmorden in 1854 is worth a peek," I said, "I've never seen it before."

"Forget it," said Angus, "let's go back."

"Oh come on Angus, we're here now. It's the opportunity of a lifetime."

"Yes, but it's my lifetime, not yours. I say go back."

I would have argued more but some local ne'er-do-well out for a stroll on the moor spotted us. He took just one look at Angus's wizardly hat, Al's "fairy" garb and long locks, and my own, no doubt, strangely androgynous appearance, and hurried away. I don't know which of us spooked him the most as he rushed back towards Hebden Bridge. Perhaps it was all of us.

"Let's hope folk don't believe the drunken fool or they'll be up here with cudgels and a priest." Remembering that he himself held holy office, Angus laughed, "If he only knew, if he only, really, knew. Come on lass, your mother's waiting. That's where we belong."

Angus found the door to the Pike more difficult to open from outside. I had come from broad daylight, and upon stepping in, the contrasting darkness made me instantly blind. Al, being last, closed the door. The aperture was no longer there, and the blackness was absolute.

"Stop messing about Al, just open the door!"

"I can't," came the thought, "it's not there."

"Here let me," Angus brushed past. "Never mind the door, there's not even a wall anymore. Hold onto each other, we don't want to get separated again."

Al held onto the reverend's shirt, and I to Al's cloak. We inched forwards in the blackness, Angus' hands in front of him, at once both eager to feel a solid surface, and at the same time fearing its impact. We saw an opening ahead. My clothing, still damp, was sticking to me. I was very happy to see that we would be emerging into bright sunlight, and I relaxed into its warmth. Turning back I expected to see the Pike, but we had come from under the broad trunk of an ancient oak.

"This is the university," I shouted. "How the hell do we get to Todmorden from here?"

"We could take a train," suggested Angus, brightening.

"Let's get moving before we're spotted," was what Al thought loudly.

Sure enough we were a sorry sight. Like us Al had dived into the pool at the Bridestones, so his clothes had got soaked, but they seemed to have dried much more completely than our own. Moreover, Angus and I had been climbing, stumbling about in the dark, and in my case falling into the mud. Looking down at myself, and across at Angus, I anticipated that other train passengers might choose to keep their distance.

"Let's go," said Angus and I began to do just that, but then I stopped. There was no library in front of me, no tower blocks behind that, no car parks or tarmac paths in sight.

"We're still in 1854," said Angus. "She's tricked us."

"Don't worry," said Al, "you'll be back before supper."

"Aye, about one hundred and thirty years before supper at this rate."

Then I had a sickening thought. "Our money is no good here! We have nothing but the clothes we're standing up in."

"I have this watch," said Angus. "Although it's not working anymore, I think it's silver." He'd actually covered the watch with his hand, reluctant to surrender the gift. "Or maybe some good Samaritan will help."

I'd done some busking, but I'd never begged for money in my life. Still, relying on charity seemed a lot kinder than parting Angus from his watch.

We walked across the expanse of landscaped garden that is Wivenhoe Park. Without the adornment of electric lamp posts, waste bins, or modern pathways, it was an unspoilt delight. It felt like late morning in midsummer and even my feet were now starting to dry out. When we got to the Colchester edge of campus there was no Greenstead estate, and no array of signposts where the roundabout should have been. I was relieved at the familiar sight of the little two-up, two-down, terraced cottages on Greenstead Road. I knew I could find the way to the station from here. It was very strange to walk along streets I knew well in which hardly a building, and certainly no shop fronts, looked familiar. As we turned a corner into what was then, as it is now, the busiest part of the precinct, Angus stopped in his tracks.

"I know exactly when we are," he exclaimed, drawing even more attention from passersby, who were thankfully keeping their distance.

In front of us was a recently constructed gothic church. It reminded me of a card in the Tarot deck. Its tower lay in pieces stacked against the surrounding buildings, many of which were also damaged.

"This is the nonconformist church in Lion Walk. Its spire fell in the great quake of '84. They've had time to start rebuilding, so it must be 1887 or '88. Do you know what this means? I can see wee Angus. I can see my son!"

As we continued walking, I knew that we were now headed to St. Mary at the Wall. Angus bore a look of grim intent, interrupted sporadically by a broad, almost insane grin. Every time the grin appeared, Al reminded him silently that there must be no interaction, that we were there only to observe. I'm not sure what Angus was thinking back at him, but Al kept repeating the instructions, and with increasing force.

When we got to the house, I confess that I was worried. Angus had quickened his pace and I'd had trouble keeping up. As he stopped by the gate to the parsonage, I could understand why he'd been reluctant to see the modern version of his garden.

Marigolds, hollyhocks, London Pride, red-hot pokers and even a few late roses were laid out in perfect symphony of colour and form.

"Wait here," he said, "we can't all be staring through the windows." It was my turn to feel the outsider.

Angus brushed himself off, took a deep breath, and then after removing his hat, smoothed down his hair before turning to face us.

"Do I look alright?"

"You appear perfectly presentable," I lied.

He walked intently towards the house, but at the last moment turned aside and approached one of the quarter-paned windows which were either side of the broad wooden door. Stooping slightly, he raised a hand to shield his eyes from the sunlight and peered inside.

"Look, he's seen her, she must be in," thought Al excitedly. Then the colour of his thinking changed. "Oh no, poor Angus! She's very much with child, but that means there's no boy yet for him to see." Al didn't give me any time to wonder how I could help my friend cope with such disappointment.

"No!" he shouted silently. "Don't do that. Don't!"

Locked into his own thoughts, Angus was already knocking on the door. A handsome young woman opened the door which seemed to have been secured by nothing more than convention.

"Good morning," she said, "can I help you? My husband's out, but if you've come for alms, I have a few pennies." There was a long silence.

"I'm no beggar." Angus was speaking slowly, choosing the words carefully. "You have to remember that your husband loved you. He wanted to come back to you. He would have given anything to see his son."

"My husband?" She noticed us behind the low wall, staring. Mistaking our looks of agonised concern, she continued, "What's happened to my husband, is he hurt, what are you telling me?"

She let the tea towel she was holding fall to the floor.

"Angus," she cried in relief, and Angus put out his arms towards her.

"Get away from my wife!" thundered the newcomer to this scene. He'd moved past us at such a pace that I'd been unaware of his arrival, right up to the moment he span Angus around, and delivered a solid punch to the poor man's head.

"Get away," he yelled, and then after gently ushering his wife in through the door, he turned to the fallen beggar.

"I'm sorry stranger, but you have no business coming here and upsetting a lady in her condition. Be off with you," and a handful of coins were placed on the ground.

"How could you be so stupid," said Al. "Irresponsible."

"Are you okay, Angus?" I cried. By now we'd rushed through the gate and were helping him to his feet.

"That is the strangest thing." Angus was speaking in a faraway voice, and I feared concussion. "I seem to have a new memory in my head," he continued, "but it feels like it's always been there. I remember landing that punch. It was a good 'un. I'm not proud of losing my temper, but the beggar was asking for it. I was so feared for my wife. Thank God Sylvie and wee Angus were alright."

"Leave the money," said Al, and I dropped the coins I had started to gather.

"But the train…" I argued lamely.

"There's no need for a train. I know exactly where we are going."

XII

Walking in silence with Al was a noisy affair. He would take any opportunity to instruct, educate, or just chatter eagerly. The trek back to Wivenhoe Park however was completed in a strange isolation. What was particularly worrying was the lack of Al's inner voice telling us not to worry. I'd grown so used to it that I now felt dreadfully alone with my own dark thoughts.

"We're early!" thought Al as we approached the oak tree. "We'll have to sit and wait."

Angus' eye was becoming a proper shiner. The skin was unbroken, but shades of purple and yellow were now appearing, much as they were across the sky. The broad horizons of Essex do sometimes allow the transition from day to night to be celebrated by a spectacular setting of the sun. In that liminal world which poets call dusk, magic happens. Shadows reach out their fingers to startle or cause fear. Bats take flight swooping too near the heads of lovers beset by midges. The desolate tone of an early owl might call out in vain for company. No wonder twilight is seen as a time when the barriers between worlds are at their most flimsy. Now one such barrier weakened, and was breached, as the ground beneath the oak's trunk opened like a giant maw, daring us to enter.

"Come on," said Angus, "let's get this over with."

Just as I had experienced on my first entry to that world, the path led us down into complete darkness, before necessitating a short but steady climb. Angus stopped in front of the wicker door.

"Not so eager to knock now, are you?" teased Al, squeezing past. Then rapping on the door he tapped out a rhythm on the sticks.

The gateway was opened. The sound of the singing, the laughing, the dozens of miniscule multi-coloured lights, and the smells of beer, food and wine all hit me at once. I wanted to stay there forever.

"Careful lass, "whispered Angus, "it's only the glamour." But it wasn't. They were all so happy to see us. Overjoyed at our return, at our victory over the goblins, at the rescue of Al.

"Are we back in the past again?" I asked.

"You're in the present," answered Al, "it's always the present."

I didn't understand, but didn't much care, for I was being carried into the Great Hall like a returning hero, borne aloft by a dozen stout arms. As they whirled and danced it made me dizzy, until I was finally lowered to the ground in the Queen's private chamber. I found my companions were beside me. Turning, I saw armed guards behind us preventing any possibility of escape.

"Step forward, Angus Munro. My, my, what has happened to your eye?"

"I punched myself, Your Majesty."

"Silence. I require no answers! Though you obviously do. Do you not know the danger in what you did? How should I answer your disobedience? Your persistent, wilful lack of any moral courage?"

"That's not fair, Your Majesty. He couldn't help himself. No human could. He needed to seek forgiveness, to prepare the woman he loved for a terrible, inexplicable loss." This outburst brought the Queen's anger my way:

"And what if she had lost the baby? Or if *her* Angus, fearing a return of the beggar, had decided not to resume his work? What if you," and she directed this at Angus with an icy power, "had failed to ever visit Faerie?"

"It would have been better for all of us." I'd never before heard one of Angus's thoughts in my head.

"How can you be so stupid? If you'd never come here, you'd never have met Robyn. In fact Robyn might never have been born. Oh yes! A million seemingly unconnected things could be changed by an extra life being injected into the past."

"But it was the life I should have had," sobbed Angus aloud.

As Al put his arms around Angus, I heard these soothing thoughts. "The life you should have had is the one you have. The love you could have given is the love you have yet to give. The man you should have been is still a child."

Angus cried then, and the Queen stepped forward. She wrapped her arms about his quaking form and sang. Her lullaby had its effect on all of us, but most assuredly on Angus. As the last notes echoed into stillness he looked into her eyes and said:

"Your Majesty. Forgive me."

"You're still not accepting it are you? I have already forgiven you." She reached down and handed him a tiny violet which Angus took to his heart.

"And now farewell to you both," said Al, "for needs be I must stay with my Queen."

"Are you in trouble?" I asked.

"Not at all - I'm her favourite," and he went and stood right next to her.

The Queen took his hand. "If only I wasn't already married to Todmer," she began. I had then a vision of the terrible ogre that we'd fled from on the moors. That must be Todmer, her husband, but how....

"Hush now! Or you'll not get home in time for supper." The Queen gestured, and the guards stood aside.

Angus and I passed through the hall as if waking from a deep slumber, reluctant to let our dream go, but also eager to tell the world.

"No lass," said Angus, reading my thoughts, "I'll never tell a soul of this. And if you're wise, you won't neither."

I thought we might get a last glimpse of the oak as we left, but the tunnel ended in a solid door set into the interior stone wall of Stoodley Pike.

"I'll be blowed," said Angus, "this thing is working again." He was referring to Dad's old watch, which told him it was only nine-thirty, so if we got a move on, we could indeed be back before eleven.

It's just as well we weren't late because Mum had waited up. I threw my arms around her as she opened the door, and over her shoulder caught the unmistakable smell of her homemade onion soup.

"You must be hungry," she said drily, and then Angus stepped into the light and Mum let out a shriek. This brought Dad running out into the hallway.

"Angus," he spluttered, "whatever's happened to your face?"

"I couldn't stop it from interacting with my fist."

Not for the first time, Mum, Dad, and myself all laughed at Angus's peculiar way of talking. It was only me though that knew just how strange the latest addition to our family really was, and I planned to keep it that way.

Epilogue

True to his word, Angus never told anyone of the many years he'd missed while underground, or about our adventure in the Colchester of 1887, nor what transpired that dark night at the Bridestones.

One afternoon, I explained to him how he could get a passport if he really wanted to discover strange lands, as he'd put it. This would have meant him changing his name to that of someone whose birth and infant death had been registered some fifty years ago.

"I have little I can call my own, but my good name, and my character, are not things that I would swap for all the tea in China," Angus had said, but he may also have become aware of the fact that by 1984 almost all strange lands had been thoroughly "discovered." Still, he was comfortable enough with my parents, and they with him. So he took on my old room and obtained an unpaid position in the local Methodist church, amazing everyone with his deep but simple understanding of all that mattered. People were sometimes surprised at his lack of knowledge, particularly modern history and current affairs. But he was an avid reader and, much to Dad's delight, even came to enjoy T.V. once he had learnt to understand the way its stories unfolded.

"What's happening now?" he'd asked, when being introduced to his first James Bond movie. "I'm sure we were in the middle of London and suddenly our hero is in the Caribbean. How did he get there so quickly?"

As for myself, the local authority and the university had taken some convincing, but I was able to take my second-year exams. There followed an idyllic summer vacation spent with Angus and the rest of my family before I went into my final year. I never returned to live with my parents after completing my degree. I had friends with a room available at a housing co-operative in London. They'd completed their degrees some three years earlier than me, and many of them lived within walking distance of each other.

Of course, I visited Todmorden often, and even had one or two more adventures up on the moors with Angus. But like him, never told anyone what happened to us, to me. Nor have I ever spoken about the realms and inhabitants of this world which are all around us but remain unseen. I've made no promise of secrecy though, so my conscience is clear in having, after all these years, put my story down for others to read. You may be tempted to ascribe it all to fantasy. My hope is that it's as true as the day is long, and as honest as the night.